Prelude

LELA GILBERT

Prelude

WORD PUBLISHING
Dallas·London·Vancouver·Melbourne

PRELUDE

Library of Congress Cataloging-in-Publication Data:

Gilbert, Lela.
   Prelude / Lela Gilbert.
      p.   cm.
   ISBN   0–8499–0968–6
   I.   Title.
PS3557.I34223P74   1992
813' .54—dc20

92–105
CIP

Printed in the United States of America

2 3 4 5 9   LB   9 8 7 6 5 4 3

To Daddy, who always kept my poems

1

The suburban street was silent but for the occasional bark of a neighborhood dog and the distant, muffled sounds of late-night television. Well past 11:30, in the back bedroom at 1715 Twelfth Avenue, a fifteen-year-old girl lay wide-awake beneath her small window, dreamily studying her hands as she turned them slowly in the leaf-patterned moonlight.

Pearly white artificial nails were carefully glued to each finger. And with all the shadows, the cracks and sores on her skin were nearly invisible. What little light there was gleamed kindly only on the fingernails, and the illusion of almost-pretty hands was really quite convincing. Even the swelling seemed to have diminished for those few magical minutes.

Then, unconsciously at first, Betty began to scratch the inside of her left elbow. The itching intensified as she dug in, and within seconds two of the beautiful nails had turned sideways and another had completely fallen off. Frustrated, she ripped away the other seven, leaving her own sharper nails free to attack the now wildly itching flesh. Before long, both arms, her neck, and her face were added to the assault.

Blood beaded in the scraped skin, and she quickly blotted it with a tissue. Betty then reached for the jar of Johnson & Johnson baby cream that she always kept close at hand. *Maybe this will keep it from sticking to my hair and nightgown,* she thought halfheartedly as she pulled her flannel sleeves down over the freshly broken wounds, hiding them in shame from her own sight.

By now a mild stinging sensation had replaced the uncontrollable itching. *So much for glamour!* she smiled wryly to herself as she gathered up the nails into a hopeless little pile. Suddenly exhausted and still trembling, she wearily began to rub at the glue that remained on her nails. Within seconds, comforted by deepening darkness, she was fast asleep.

The slam of locker doors. Laughing, shouting teenage voices. Clicking heels and scuffling tennis shoes. Friday brought its own excitement to Glen Oaks High School, because fall was in the air, and fall meant football. Betty Fuller was an avid fan of the local high school team. Despite the fact that she didn't really have a group of special school friends to which she belonged, she rarely missed a Friday night game.

"Hey, Fullerbrush Lizzie! Got a date for the game?"

"Shut up, Larry!" Scowling her disapproval, one of the green-and-white clad cheerleaders angrily nudged the tease. "Honestly! Can't you ever be nice?"

Betty cringed at the remark, rubbing self-consciously at the glue that still clung to her stubby nails. She knew full well how the boys at school would feel about taking her out. Besides the burned, peeling skin on her face, neck, and limbs and the cracked knuckles on her hands, she was a little overweight and dressed— well, she was just a misfit. That's all there was to it.

Yet, somehow, in spite of the way she appeared to others, Betty Fuller knew she was all wrong. She was a bright girl, curiously philosophical. And her sharp, sarcastic wit frequently surprised anyone who sat close enough to her in class to hear the cynical asides she muttered under her breath.

Why didn't she change her style? Well, where would she start? Her day began, centered, and ended with her "condition."

It controlled her life. She couldn't think past its limitations. She tried not to be too obvious about scratching, but the fact was she was always scratching. Meanwhile, she had to hide her legs under textured stockings. She had to hide her arms under long sleeves, her neck under turtlenecks and scarves, her face under pancake makeup. She could only hope that her artfully applied mascara would draw attention toward her clear blue eyes and away from all her other visual faults. The glasses she was supposed to be wearing were deliberately left in her purse. Things were bad enough without glasses. *If everyone else's flaws are a blur to me, maybe my flaws will be a blur to them, too. I think I like the world better blurry.* She smiled at the image of being a sort of pink fog to the eyes of the student body.

A pep rally was about to begin in the gym, and she hurried to gather her books from the locker before making her way there. Once the rally was over she would head for home, avoiding the after-school crowds and any further comments from the boys.

Looking around the crowded gymnasium, Betty spotted Miriam Paar sitting alone on the bleachers. As always, not the trace of a smile creased her face. *She's such a sourpuss,* Betty reminded herself in disgust. Nevertheless, she sat down beside the skinny redhead.

"God! How I hate pep rallies. They are so *infantile.* All this so-called school spirit is nothing but a pretense!" So said Miriam, and Betty sighed and shook her head. The fact was, having friends by default was better than having no friends at all. Besides, Miriam's brother Eddie was a folk singer, drove a red sports car, and seemed almost eccentric enough to be a Bohemian. Surely Miriam, too, had some spark of redeeming social quality.

"Oh, no! I love pep rallies! They're fun! Wouldn't you want to be a cheerleader if you were popular enough?" Betty felt almost weak contemplating such an achievement.

Miriam somehow managed to look even more miserable. Her small, pinched face took yet another expression of disgust, and her voice was sharp. "Please, Betty! Don't insult me. I wouldn't *want* to be popular enough. I'd be humiliated if people believed that I would even *consider* being a cheerleader."

Betty was relieved when their conversation was drowned out by the thunderous roar of foot-stomping, hand-clapping, and rhythmic syllables. The football team had entered the gym. Her face ached with smiles. Secretly she watched number 84 very closely. His name was Billy Browning, and for three years she'd quietly coveted his attention.

Billy was no beauty himself. But acne was a more acceptable disfigurement than the endless cycle of itching, bleeding, and scaling that endlessly tormented Betty. Eczema. Chronic dermatitis. Skin allergy. None of her doctors called it by the same name. They did agree, however, that no medication or treatment regimen had ever done it a bit of good.

Anyway, she'd sat next to Billy in eighth grade and he'd grudgingly told her, "Well, you're a little pretty . . ."

Since that day, she'd loved him with all her heart.

"THUNDER, THUNDER, THUNDERATION . . . WE'RE THE WILDCAT CONGREGATION . . . WE ARE FILLED WITH JUBILATION . . . WE ARE OUT TO WIN THE NATION!"

Lost in the crowd's synergy, the girl was temporarily free of herself as her voice joined the tide of sound that swelled toward the rafters of the sweat-smelling building. She clapped and cheered and felt lighthearted with the idea that, this time, the Lorenzo High School Bears would be absolutely defeated, embarrassed, and trashed by her green-and-white heroes.

And Lord, please let Billy catch a pass and score. I know it would mean a lot to him . . . A brief fantasy caused her to be a little slow getting to her feet for the alma mater. A flush of embarrassment engulfed her, and sweat stung her sore face. Had anyone seen? She scowled, hoping no one was looking at her. Where was Miriam Paar, anyway? Probably in the bathroom smoking. Mercifully, the moment quickly passed, and as the pep rally ended,

Betty vanished into the crowd, her heart filled with visions of the coming game, her imagination painting richly colored scenes of gridiron glory.

Harold M. Fuller was an ex-marine sergeant. He operated heavy equipment on road construction projects and proudly served as a church deacon. He was a ruddy, sandy-haired man, three inches shorter than his daughter and forever puzzled by her. A sophomore in high school, she was already better educated than he was, and he resented her questioning his dogma. He was generally gruff with her, found it impossible to compliment her, yet saw some strange strength in her eyes. Most of all, her overwhelming physical problems saddened him. Was her continuous struggle somehow his fault?

"Can't we sit in the cheering section, Daddy?"

"It's too noisy!" he shot back, heading for the top of the stands at the forty-yard line. *You are OLD, Daddy. Old and boring.* Her annoyance was, of course, balanced by the fact that her father was her only means of getting to the game. Nevertheless, he was bull-headed and never seemed to understand the way she felt. Worse yet, he didn't seem to care.

The two of them did share a love for football, though, and Harold was glad to spend his autumn Friday evenings with his daughter. His diminutive wife Lucilla was equally glad to have a few hours to herself, meticulously preparing her notes for the Sunday school lessons she taught each week. *If she were a man, she'd be a preacher!* Harold reflected with pride, as he envisioned her standing straight and stern before the admiring class. *She needs time to get herself ready. There's always some troublemaker there questioning her. Why can't they just let her teach?*

He was just beginning to feel a surge of defensive anger for Lucilla when Betty interrupted his reverie, nudging him as Billy Browning rumbled across the field with the other players. Harold was aware of his daughter's long-term crush on the homely tight end. *Why on earth . . . ?* Teenage girls had been a mystery to him since his days as a pimply faced high school dropout. And this offspring of his was the strangest yet.

Unfortunately, this particular game was a less triumphant exercise than Betty had imagined. The Lorenzo High School Bears featured an all-star offense and a new coach. Toward the end of the first quarter, Harold began to long for the USC Trojans or the L.A. Rams. Anybody, really. The Glen Oaks Wildcats were losing disgracefully, and there was absolutely no salvation in sight. "Let's head out of here . . ." he muttered during the fourth quarter. "At least we'll miss the traffic."

"Not before the alma mater!" His daughter looked at him in despair. How could he?

Nevertheless they left, and she quietly wiped the tears from her eyes as she trailed behind him, looking back with longing at the chalk-striped field, the Wildcat fight song fading into the crisp, smoke-scented September night.

Sunday morning arrived cloaked in fog, which would burn off by noon into smoggy, gray humidity. Betty's two concerns before going out the door to church were to have thoroughly practiced her piano offertory and to have battled her appearance into submission. In actuality, the offertory paled in significance to the cosmetic struggle, an unhappy matter that threatened to destroy, once and for all, the last vestige of her self-esteem.

She frowned at her hair. Her barbershop haircut hit her long chin line awkwardly, but somehow it didn't seem too bad today. She picked her dull blonde frizz one last time before layering it with hair spray. The scent of spray that filled the bathroom gave her a twinge of confidence. Not a single baby-fine hair would move once she was finished!

She studied herself in the mirror, searching for more flaws needing to be plastered with makeup. The face that stared back at her was high-cheekboned and even featured, and the blue eyes would have looked large if the eyelids hadn't been so swollen. Betty had painstakingly penciled brown eyebrows over her own nearly invisible ones, giving an unappealing hardness to her expression. The pale, frosty lipstick dictated by teenage fashion served only to accent the redness of her skin. None of these things were clear to her, however. Her mind was focused only on covering the blemishes—the rest was a constant source of discouragement—day after day, month after month.

Even with all her imperfections, that particular Sunday, wearing a bright pink dress that just brushed her knees, her teased hairdo somewhat under control, Betty felt just the slightest bit attractive, comparatively speaking, of course. This unusual sensation made her smile a little more, and smiling had a way of unknitting her brow. The effect was an improvement.

"Are you ready?" Lucilla's voice was harsh with impatience. Neither she nor Harold could understand their daughter's ceaseless efforts in front of the mirror. Both of them were approaching fifty, and such adolescent vanity eluded their empathy. To their way of thinking, being on time was far more important than the finishing touches on a hopelessly marred countenance. Church leaders should not arrive late.

"No one's going to be looking at you anyway," Lucilla announced for the thousandth time in Betty's life. "We'll be in the car!" She tucked her well-worn Bible next to her handbag and slammed the door as she went out. As was his habit, Harold had already "warmed up the engine" and was waiting irritably for his wife and daughter. Sunday mornings were notoriously tense at the Fuller house.

Bethany Baptist Church was a dun-colored stucco affair, inexpensively constructed in an also-shabby neighborhood. Its sanctuary seated about two hundred people, but no more than seventy-five ever showed up at once. Those who did appear each Sunday always sat in the same places, with the same posture and the same fixed expressions. It was an unspoken breach of etiquette to take the seat of another Bethany regular. And it was up to the ushers to see that no uninformed visitors, rare as they were, were seated in the wrong place.

Sunday school began in the sanctuary, and Betty sat at the piano, playing the same choruses that she played every week. It would have been boring to her, but she knew all four songs with her eyes closed, right down to the small flourishes she had long ago improvised between measures. Considering all her other insecurities, virtuosity was far more expedient than variety.

Her piano playing, like Lucilla's teaching and Harold's political position in the church, provided Betty with a certain acceptability that she lacked at school. Bethany Baptist Church was several miles from Glen Oaks High School, and none of her young acquaintances attended both, so she was able to project a slightly different persona at church. Her intelligence and family background gave her a bit of an edge in biblical matters. After all, Lucilla Fuller's daughter would always know the right answers. And she really wasn't all that bad at the piano. The real truth was that the odd collection of people who remained in that dreary church were not much more socially desirable than she was. And as any one of them might sagely observe, misery loves company.

So it was that Betty Fuller liked church. Furthermore, besides her continuing intrigue with number 84 on the Wildcat football team, she was keenly aware that Jerry Baldwin, the church organist, had gorgeous blue eyes and sometimes laughed at her jokes. Yes, church was better than school. More significantly, it was far more important to her parents, and therefore it was important to her, too. She wanted desperately to please Mother and Daddy, more than she could even admit to herself.

When the morning worship service began, she scanned the bulletin to see if her name was spelled correctly. Once her offertory performance was completed (with only two minor mistakes), she gratefully entered an oblivious state that would make the hour-long service pass a little more quickly.

Private daydreams carried her beyond the ugly pews, beyond the droned announcements and the off-key vocal rendition of "The New Jerusalem." Betty heard precious little of Rev. Orville P. Turner's sermon, which would be thoroughly dissected later on that day anyway. Instead, she painted herself into portraits of affection. She heard whispered words of tenderness. She rehearsed entrances into sunlit rooms, where love awaited her. Lost in imaginings, a quiet smile spontaneously curved her mouth, giving her a certain spiritual aura. Most Bethany members would have confidently described her as a "nice Christian girl."

Now and then something the pastor said would momentarily interrupt her thoughts. Her eyes squinted him into focus behind the blonde wood of the pulpit. What was he saying? Oh, yes. Baptism. Had he mentioned baptism? A memory drifted through her mind. Seven years before, she had donned a white gown, had taken the hand of the distinguished minister of their former church (they had left over some doctrinal dispute), and had stepped into the tepid baptistry waters, trembling from head to foot. She had hardly been able to get her voice to answer his quiet question: "Do you, Elisabeth Fuller, wish to follow Jesus for the rest of your life?" A feeble, quaking "Yes . . ." was all she had been able to manage. The melody of an old hymn, "Where He Leads Me I Will Follow," had wafted toward her from the organ and the softly singing congregation. *Following Jesus.* A larger emotion than she could contain had swelled in her child's heart— something more vast than her nine-year-old understanding could comprehend. *Following Jesus.* Despite the fact that her skin had stung unmercifully from the water and that her gown was stuck to her shaking legs, she knew beyond any doubt that she had done "the right thing." She had followed Jesus into the waters of baptism, and the joy of it had drenched her face with tears.

Now new tears stung her eyes at the recollection. Vaguely she wondered what this Sunday morning at Bethany Baptist Church had to do with that overwhelming moment. She had never seen a great deal of practicality in the practice of religion as she'd observed it. Faith seemed to be an intellectual matter—a matter of facts, opinions, and "good, sound doctrine." Without fail, Bibles were read daily and prayers were offered regularly. But tempers still flared. Tongues still wagged. Frustration reigned, disappointment prevailed, and no one really seemed to care. Jesus seemed farther away than even two thousand years of history should have carried him.

Betty scratched her neck, then her leg. Her thoughts made her uncomfortable. They seemed rebellious. Daydreams were far less disagreeable than hard questions anyway, and fortunately church was over.

Voices joined in an unenthusiastic closing hymn, "Blest be the tie that binds our hearts in Christian love . . ." Considering what she'd heard at home about several members of the congregation, their hearts were bound very loosely indeed, Christian love notwithstanding. Betty smirked at her little joke and strained her eyes to see if by some chance Jerry Baldwin was looking her way from the organ bench. He wasn't. She avoided the pastor who was greeting his flock at the door, not wanting him to have to touch her rough, scabby hand.

Heading toward the car, she said polite good-byes to half a dozen familiar faces wearing Sunday morning smiles. She scratched her arm impatiently as she waited for Harold and Lucilla to complete their very serious discussion with the church trustees.

I wish they'd hurry up . . . she grumbled silently. Instead of driving back to their house as usual, they would be going to see Grandma and Grandpa in Garden Grove. It wasn't the most exciting place to spend a Sunday afternoon, but it was certainly better than sitting around at home. And her rumbling stomach reminded her that Grandma's fried chicken was the best anywhere.

Meanwhile, an unrelenting sun was smoldering through the smog, and naturally Harold had left the car securely locked. Absently she began to rub her cheek, then her ear. It was miserably hot and her skin always itched more when it was sweaty. All things considered, Betty wanted to get in the car, roll down the window, and be on her way.

"Orville has *never* been really firm about eternal security," Lucilla complained as the well-tuned Ford carried them toward their Garden Grove destination. "He's wishy-washy. And I think it's because old Detwieler has him wrapped around his little finger. Orville's afraid he'll lose Detwieler's money, and Detwieler's a *Methodist*."

Harold nodded his head in agreement. "Orville is never firm about anything controversial. He plays into the Methodists' hands. He plays into the Pentecostals' hands. Did you hear what he said about tongues?"

"I was *disgusted!*" Lucilla spat the words out with vehemence. "He's so afraid to take a stand against anything!" She paused dramatically. "And he *knows* better!"

"I'm going to talk to William and old man Hetrick. We need to confront him at the deacons' meeting Friday night."

"What did he say about tongues? I must have missed it." Betty was curious.

"He said *some people believe* that 1 Corinthians 13:8 says that the speaking in unknown tongues has ceased in this dispensation. He's afraid to say dogmatically that tongues are wrong."

"Maybe he's not sure . . ." The daughter had never quite understood the gravity of this issue as her mother perceived it.

"*Of course* he's sure. He's just wishy-washy. I'm going to tell him how Helen Brown is trying to infiltrate my Sunday school class with her pentecostalism. Maybe then he'll see how he'd better take a stand! They'll take over his church and he'll lose it! That's the way *they* operate!"

Lucilla was growing increasingly agitated and Betty knew better than to ask more questions. She would be seen as an adversary, and she didn't mean to be one. "How did my offertory sound?" she asked timidly.

"It was fine. You made a couple of mistakes, but I don't think they were too obvious."

"Anyway, Harold," Lucilla was not to be distracted from her focus. "I think it *is* time Orville was confronted. It's as if he expects me to take a firm stand in Sunday school, and then he's soft in the pulpit. I'm sick and tired of it."

The conversation continued until Grandma's house was in sight. The chicken, mashed potatoes, and corn-on-the-cob were as delicious as ever and provided a final conclusion to the critique of the pastor.

"You didn't bring me a berry pie?" Grandpa's eyes twinkled as he hugged Lucilla. She looked happy and pleased. A real love had grown between Harold's father and Lucilla, and they enjoyed each other immensely. He always teased her about bringing him a pie, recalling some long-forgotten incident.

"I promise to bring you my absolute best berry pie the very next time we come!"

"You make the best berry pies on earth!" he cooed.

She's so sweet sometimes, Betty thought, watching her mother and Grandpa talking merrily across the food-laden table. *It's like she's two different people—she's the Sunday school teacher one time and she's just plain Lucilla the next. I love her when she's like this. But she's so . . . well, I guess she's kind of hard sometimes . . .*

Grandma, on the other hand, was not especially fond of Lucilla, and as far as she was concerned, Betty was a disaster. She was rather proud of Marlene and Debbie, her other two granddaughters. They were about the same age, had limitless boyfriends, and wore the most stylish clothes.

How typical of Lucilla to have a child like Betty and then to dress her like a frump. Grandma studied the mother and daughter disapprovingly. *I don't know what Harold sees in her. She's such a religious fanatic.* Not that Grandma claimed to be on anyone's best-dressed list herself. But she had eyes, didn't she?

After cleaning up the dishes, the Harold Fuller family settled into the sagging but comfortable living room sofas. Grandma and Grandpa sank into their matching recliners.

"How's your sister Abigail doing, Lucilla?" Grandma asked sweetly. Lucilla's older sister Abigail was a spinster missionary in Kenya and was not a happy subject to any of the Fullers. Harold felt that Abigail had always been unreasonably critical of Lucilla, producing a lifetime of hurt feelings. The very mention of Abigail's name made him feel defensive for his wife.

Lucilla thought Abigail was too health conscious and narrow-minded about such worldly matters as lipstick, nail polish, and drinking coffee. She felt she had the right to defy her sister, but had never done so without a twinge of guilt.

Although Harold and Lucilla had logged many years of disliking Abigail for countless reasons, Betty actually held the biggest grudge of all against her. First of all, there was something about Abigail's career that threatened Betty's fragile spirituality. The sweetness of her baptismal experience seemed to clash with the harsh reality of Aunt Abigail's severe commitment. Going to Africa as a missionary seemed like the capstone of Baptist religion— if you really, truly decided to "Follow Jesus," Africa is precisely where you'd end up. You'd be strange. You'd be unattractive. And you'd be reluctantly admired for your consecrated life.

Worse than that was the implication of Aunt Abigail's image. She, like Betty, had always been a misfit. They shared the same chin, the same nose, and the same coloring. Everyone knew that Abigail was ugly, fat, and nearsighted. (Of course she *always* wore her glasses.) Furthermore, she had such an abrasive personality that she'd never found a place for herself in the "real world." It seemed that only the wildest savages in the deepest heart of darkest Africa could tolerate her.

"Betty, dear . . ."

Before Grandma could say another word, Betty braced herself. She knew exactly what to expect. She was angry before the words reached her ears.

". . . someday I believe you'll be a missionary, too. I think God will call you to His service. You could really make a place for yourself in Africa. You're the spitting image of Abigail, you know."

"I'm not anything like Abigail," she protested, fighting for control of her tears, believing herself that the two of them were exactly the same. Her voice grew shaky as her panic increased. "And I don't want to be a missionary."

"And another thing," she spluttered, trying to make at least one valid, unemotional point, "I could never go anywhere with skin like mine. I'd die of an infection. They'd never take me, even if I wanted to go."

"I'm sure they could find a place for you, dear," Grandma smiled kindly. "They take all kinds of people . . ."

"I *hate* missionaries!" Betty suddenly choked out bitter words, frantically covering her ears with her hands. Desperately, she wanted to behave properly, to do the right thing. She could not. Avoiding the shocked eyes of both her parents, she stormed out of the room. "I *hate* Abigail and I *hate* Africa . . . I will *never be a missionary in Africa!*" By now she was screaming.

She slammed the bathroom door and locked it. Collapsing on the green carpeting next to the bathtub, she wept uncontrollably for nearly half an hour.

2

Wrapped in a quilted red robe, Betty lay in front of the fireplace for the third day in a row, tranquilized by the warmth against her back. In the next room, Lucilla and Harold were playing Scrabble with Charles and Emma Baird.

The snapping fire and a steady stream of friendly banter were the only sounds Betty could hear. Outside there was silence. It was nearly Christmas, and the elder Fullers had decided to spend the holidays in the Southern California mountains. Apart from relatives, the Bairds were their only friends and were also the proud owners of a weekend mountain cabin. What better place to spend Christmas?

It was a frigid, brittle December, with temperatures in the mid-twenties. Clear skies held no promise of snow. In fact, the air was remarkably dry, and consequently Betty's skin was in a miserable state. Each crease and fold was cracked and bloody, and a powdery cloud of dry flakes followed her every movement. Apart from the discomfort, she didn't feel well anyway. A persistent sleepiness had rendered her nearly immobile. For some reason she was finding it hard to concentrate.

This particular Christmas season offered no pleasant distractions, either. The Bairds' white plastic tree, adorned with silver balls, was continuously bathed in ever-changing pastel hues, thanks to a revolving, multicolored floodlight. "No needles on the floor, and no fire danger!" Emma proudly announced as the little tree was being assembled, branch by branch, in the corner of the knotty pine living room.

It suits you, Emma, Betty had grumbled to herself, watching the proceedings from her fireplace haven. *Fifty-year-old women certainly are a breed unto themselves.*

Christmas nostalgia had touched her only once that year, and fleetingly at that. During a brief walk along a tree-lined path, she had trudged ankle-deep in pine needles. Fighting drowsiness, that short stroll had nearly expended her meager energy, but it had also filled her with the cool breath of a thousand evergreens. Some fresh-cut tree, sparkling with multicolored ornaments, stirred within her memory and then vanished just as quickly.

Christmas morning she was presented with two cheerless gifts—the kind of sensible school clothing items that Lucilla was happy to sew. *You're ungrateful!* Betty chided herself as she set the boxes aside with a quiet, "Thank you. How nice."

Meanwhile, Lucilla, Harold, and the Bairds were thoroughly enjoying the fact that they had bought each other identical selections of See's chocolates. That coincidence was of no benefit to Betty whatsoever. Someone had decided ages back that all her favorite foods—chocolate, tomatoes, eggs, and milk—were "bad" for her skin. She knew better, because for years she'd bartered her unwanted school lunch items for forbidden delicacies. Naturally she kept the results of her tests private. Why argue?

The day after Christmas Betty slept all the way home. A scalding shower stopped a sudden bout of itching. Relieved, she smeared a thick layer of baby cream over every inch of her skin, and by 8:30 in the evening she was lying limp in her bed. In the background she heard snatches of an old nostalgic standard, "You Belong to Me," wafting her way from the television: "Fly the ocean in a silver plane . . . Watch the jungle when it's wet with rain . . ."

That song had never failed to arouse some indefinable long-ing within her. But at that moment, there was no way she could propel herself back into the living room to listen.

This continuing tiredness had begun weeks before, and she had missed several days of school. Those mornings Betty had felt unable to complete the exhausting project of getting herself dressed, made up, and gathering her unfinished homework only to encounter the inevitable social unpleasantness. A certain guilt accompanied her lethargy, because the problem seemed more emotional than physical. Either way, she hadn't been to school.

Tonight she was beginning to wonder about herself. Bed felt all too comfortable. Absently she started to scratch her arm. She was startled to feel something strange on her raw skin, some sort of hard, sore pimples. She turned on the light, and with a sinking sense of horror, saw peculiar red bumps on both arms.

Boy, there's nothing like a little dry mountain air, she thought bleakly, fighting an unfamiliar fear that something was seriously wrong. *Oh well. It's just a new version of the same old thing.* Betty tried to comfort herself. The dread persisted.

Next morning, her face bore silent evidence that a new, violent reaction had occurred somewhere inside her young body. Angry eruptions had spread across her neck and cheeks. Her scalp was excruciatingly sore to the touch, covered with lumps.

"Mother, look at this."

Lucilla said nothing, but her frown was deeper than usual. Harold had left for work, and she had no car. Was this a serious problem or not? Was is worth calling the one taxicab in town to get to the doctor? She hesitated before dialing.

Christmas decorations still shimmered in the breeze, sus-pended across Glen Oaks' main street. With Lucilla's help, Betty got out of the cab as quickly as possible, hoping no one would see her. She wore the ubiquitous red robe, which by now was stained with baby cream and speckles of blackened blood. After a brief examination, the doctor was frowning even more intensely than Lucilla. High fever. Low blood pressure. Outrageously rapid pulse.

By sunset, Betty had been admitted to Queen of Heaven Hospital. By 8:00 that night, she was barely conscious. From her view, the nuns who came and went from the room were imaginatively transforming themselves into strange shapes and sizes. Their black-and-white clad personages first resembled seagulls, then ghouls, then gentle-eyed women with worried faces.

By now Betty's eyes were nearly swollen shut, and the boil-like condition that covered her body was dreadfully sore to the touch. *At least I don't itch,* she reminded herself during a lucid moment, while the delirium briefly ebbed. But in fact she did itch at times, and when she scratched, blood no longer beaded. It spurted from the abscesses.

The nurses tied her hands and feet to the bed. Late in the night, Houdini-like, she escaped, feebly making her way to the toilet.

"You stay in that bed, young lady!" They restrained her again, this time more firmly. Too weak to fight, she submitted.

"What's wrong with me?" she whispered to Lucilla.

"I don't know . . . they think it's just a bad allergy attack, so they've started giving you cortisone. But Dr. Petrowski isn't so sure." Dr. Petrowski was an allergist, unlike the general practitioner who had hospitalized her.

"Why am I tied up?"

"Because you keep scratching."

From the time of earliest childhood, both Betty's parents had said at least a hundred times a day, "Don't scratch! Stop your scratching!" Unavoidably, she had disobeyed. Yet despite the impossibility of their instructions, a never-ending sense of guilt prevailed.

They said "Stop." She kept scratching until she was raw and sore and bleeding. Was the whole miserable situation somehow the result of her disobedience?

Betty drifted in and out of sleep, waking up to the same torturous discomfort she'd left behind. A pair of visitors came into focus—Bill Klinert, the Bethany Baptist youth pastor, and his pregnant wife Gloria. Betty squinted to see them, but before she could say hello, Gloria was being carried out of the room. She'd taken one look at Betty and passed out.

"Mother, do I really look that sickening?"

"It doesn't matter how you look, Betty. That's not what we're worried about. Besides, Gloria's pregnant. Everything makes you sick when you're pregnant."

"When will Daddy be here?"

"Saturday. He's staying on the job this week. Now go back to sleep."

After the first seventy-two hours in the hospital, Betty's high fever submitted to medication. The surges of delirium were stilled. But the skin's ongoing devastation persisted, uncontrolled.

Dr. Petrowski visited every day. A slight, graying doctor with a European accent, he would hesitantly enter the room, politely check Betty's pulse, listen to her chest, then call Lucilla outside. Betty noticed the weariness in her mother's face. She'd hardly ever left her daughter's side.

She loves me in her own way. She just doesn't like me sometimes.

One day, while Lucilla and Dr. Petrowski talked outside the door, Rev. Orville P. Turner appeared, gravely greeting Betty. He stayed less than five minutes at her side, hardly knowing what to say, murmuring something about Job and his troubles.

"Read to me about Job," Betty said, nodding toward Lucilla's Bible which she had left on the bedside table. He picked it up, glad for the familiar sensation of thumbing through its well-worn pages.

". . . And the Lord said unto Satan, Behold, he is in thine hand; but save his life.

"So went Satan forth from the presence of the Lord, and smote Job with sore boils from the sole of his foot unto his crown.

"And he took him a potsherd to scrape himself withal; and he sat down among the ashes."

Betty interrupted, "What's a potsherd?"

"Well, I believe it's a piece of broken pottery."

"Do you know why he was scraping himself?"

"No, I'm not sure . . ."

"I do. He was itching. And he couldn't scratch hard enough to stop it."

Rev. Turner stared at her, at a loss for words. He replaced the Bible on the table, careful not to knock over the water pitcher. Before leaving, he asked Betty if she would like to have "a word of prayer." She nodded. His conversational tone suddenly changed, and his voice seemed to lower dramatically. Even the pronunciation of his words was transformed as he began to pray.

"Our Heavenly Father, how we thank Thee for Thy constant watch and care over ourselves and our loved ones. We come before Thee now here in this hospital, beseeching Thee for Thy help. Lord, we ask that Thou mightst lay Thy hand of healing upon Betty, and that Thou wouldst comfort her family. We ask these favors in Jesus' name, Amen."

His voice normalized again, Orville P. reached out to squeeze Betty's tied hand. Before he could stop himself, he recoiled. He patted her arm instead, which was safely hidden under the sheet.

I don't blame him for not touching me. I'll bet Job's friends didn't want to touch him either.

Rev. Turner walked out of the room and joined the now-animated exchange between Lucilla and the doctor. Betty could hear her mother's voice complaining about the hospital's Mother Superior and her "domineering attitude." She smiled vaguely to herself. Only an inflexible, incontestable health insurance policy could have ever placed Lucilla Fuller and her daughter within the confines of a staunchly Roman Catholic hospital at the mercy of an entire convent of nuns. After that particular conversation, Betty noticed that the nuns no longer visited her.

When Lucilla came back into the room, Betty told her about Job. "I think maybe he had the same thing I have."

Lucilla's desire for absolute biblical accuracy was momentarily overshadowed by compassion for her only child. She paused, tears glistening in her eyes, then spoke kindly, "Well, Betty, if you'll read the whole book, you'll find out that God gave Job back more than he lost after all his troubles were over. Maybe He'll do the same for you."

"When is Daddy coming?"

"I told you before. He'll be here on the weekend. He's staying on the job this week."

As days passed, baths in a purple solution of potassium permanganate caused Betty's stubbornly disfigured skin to look, if possible, even worse. The chemical dyed her body a weird brown color and darkened every lesion. Meanwhile, her hair was falling out in clumps.

Kimberly, a kind-hearted black nurses' aide, helped her out of the tub one morning. "You are too skinny, girl!" she scowled with concern. "We've got to get you fattened up a little!"

Betty sighed, pleased that Kimberly had noticed something besides her blemishes. "I know. There isn't much left of me, is there? I only weighed 105 pounds this morning, and at 5-foot-8 that's ridiculous."

Kimberly shook her head, wondering if the girl would live long enough to regain the twenty or twenty-five pounds she'd lost.

Every day, just after breakfast, Betty was faithfully visited by an elderly Irish patient, who was recuperating from back surgery. He was in evident pain and moved at a snail's pace. But he never failed to say the same words to Betty, morning by morning. "Child, you've got a pretty wee nose, do you know that? You've got the prettiest little nose I've ever seen." He always came to see her. He always smiled. And a faint trace of hope always remained after he left.

"I get the point, Mr. Murphy," Betty laughed at him one day. "My nose is the only thing on my body that isn't covered in boils."

"Well don't you worry, child. The rest will be pretty too someday. You just wait and see!"

She hadn't paid much attention to Rev. Turner's prayer. But Mr. Murphy's promise lodged in her heart to stay.

Five weeks after she was first admitted, Betty was still in the hospital. By now she was extraordinarily thin and could barely walk. Only one friend her own age had visited her throughout the course of her illness. Jody Gardiner, from Bethany Baptist Church of course, had shown up on a Sunday afternoon. One look at Betty, and she too had all but fainted, reeling for the door in retreat. *She's faking it.* Betty thought bitterly. *She heard about Gloria Klienert, so she thought she'd faint too. She's always trying to be dramatic. What a phony.*

"See you later! Tell everybody hi!" Betty called out after Jody, ignoring her plight.

As the days passed, Betty battled with her physical condition while a frustrated Dr. Petrowski struggled with the medical conundrum. Determined to resolve the matter once and for all, he doggedly stayed awake for more than twenty-four hours, poring over every book he owned on skin disorders. Before daybreak, he had the answer. Betty's problem wasn't eczema at all! It was some sort of an infection.

He briskly ordered new tests. His theory was quickly verified by the positive results of a series of blood and skin cultures—staphylococcal bacteria was the culprit. "My God!" he chastised himself. "All that cortisone. It's a miracle we didn't kill her!" Penicillin was prescribed instantaneously.

"We won't be able to put an anesthetic in the medication, because you might be allergic to it," the doctor explained, his heavily accented voice apologetic. "And Betty, the shots may sting a little."

Sting they did. As a matter of fact, every intermuscular injection caused Betty's upper legs to cramp agonizingly, sometimes convulsing with pain. And to her dismay she had to have four injections a day. She hid her head under the pillow to stifle her screams. She bit holes in several pillowcases. Every time a nurse walked into the room, tears came too.

"No—not you again!" she'd shudder, trying to disguise her fear with a mock horror and whatever humor she could muster. The fact was, she was terrified, and most of the nurses tried every possible way to alleviate her suffering. Some gave the shots quickly, others took nearly five minutes. Some divided the medication into two shots, one in each side, others gave them halfway down the thigh. By the time ten days had passed, when Betty tried to walk, her legs simply could not support her weight.

The decision was made to try intravenous antibiotics. Two more weeks passed, and still the daily cultures came back positive. Apparently the strain of bacteria was penicillin-resistant and had formed a colony in a heart valve. Infection was being pumped throughout her body with every irregular pulse beat.

As a last resort, a drug called chloromycetin was introduced, amid great fears of lethal side effects. It was effective against staphylococcal infections, but equally notorious for causing irreversible blood damage—a condition called aplastic anemia.

Fortunately the drastic measure had favorable results, and Betty's red blood cells valiantly survived the assault. Valentine's Day found her getting ready to go home after nearly eight weeks of hospitalization.

Pulling on a new pair of black slacks and a white cotton turtleneck, she made her way to the mirror, scrutinizing herself critically. Her skin was blotched with various shades of purple and pink, but it didn't appear to be scarred and wasn't particularly broken out, at least for the moment. The hair that had fallen out during the worst weeks of the sickness was growing back in around the sides of her face, blonder than before and a little wavy.

Well, where there's life there's hope.

She thought of Mr. Murphy who had long since gone home. What would he say now?

It's just as well he left. He'd probably be disappointed.

Several hours before Harold and Lucilla arrived to take their fragile daughter home, a candy striper handed Betty a couple of greeting cards that had come in the hospital mail. One was from Jerry Baldwin, the church organist. The printed text read, "If you would get well, we could make beautiful music together." It was signed "Love, Jerry."

Betty knew very well that Mrs. Baldwin, Jerry's kind-hearted mother, had picked out the card. She also knew very well that the card's sentiment had nothing to do with romance, but related to Jerry and Betty's organ and piano duets, which they sometimes played during the Sunday morning service.

No matter. Fantasy prevailed. By afternoon, Betty had re-lived every smile Jerry had ever sent her way from the organ bench. Every time she visualized the word "love" at the bottom of the card, scrawled in his own hand, a pleasant sensation rippled inside her. She examined his signature again and again, trying to make the feeling come back.

The memory of number 84, Billy Browning, grew fainter with every passing hour. By the end of the day, Betty was impossibly in love with Jerry Baldwin.

She glanced through the hospital room window at a flowering tree, blushing pink with the promise of buds. Just then Daddy walked into the room to take her home.

Winter was over.

She couldn't wait to get back to church.

The white cottage slumbered beneath blankets of morning fog, embraced by a crimson bougainvillaea. Inside, Lucilla's coffee percolated fragrantly on the kitchen counter, while Betty tried to decide which sweatshirt to wear.

Months had passed since Betty's discharge from Queen of Heaven Hospital. Tutors had guided her through the last semester of school, and now, at long last, summer vacation had arrived.

Not going to school had been a blessed relief. Without all the social stresses that usually distracted her, she had done better in her studies than ever before. And now, miles away from Glen Oaks and Bethany Baptist Church, pleasant days surely lay ahead. Even life without Jerry Baldwin's rare organ-bench smiles didn't seem so bad that morning.

In an effort to move as close to the ocean as possible, Harold and Lucilla had serendipitously located an inexpensive rental just a block from one of Laguna Beach's most spectacular coves. Dr. Petrowski had suggested ocean air, sun, and saltwater as a possible treatment for Betty's eczema. As usual, Harold would be away at work except on weekends. So apart from the financial commitment, the three-month experiment was no burden to Lucilla. The woman's gentle side hungered for the sea.

So it was that in early June, mother and daughter left the cottage before 9:00 A.M. and set off to explore their new surroundings. They hurried past Victoria Drive's gingerbread houses and dazzling gardens, turning left at the public stairway leading to the beach below.

Betty's few pleasant childhood memories all seemed to be set against a backdrop of California beaches. Sunsets at Newport. Picnics at Corona del Mar. Songs sung around a campfire at Huntington. Her very earliest recollection was of Harold carrying her across a pale stretch of sand, silvery waves ruffling alongside them. When she reminded him, he always said, "Oh, yeah, that was the Silver Strand at San Diego." To her, it had been pure joy.

A long descent led them to the last concrete stair and onto the sand. Not a soul was on the broad beach to their left. They turned to the right and stepped over a stone crevasse. As they made their way around a rocky corner, Betty caught her breath.

Just ahead, vine-draped cliffs soared skyward from the rugged beach, crowned by exquisite homes and cascading flowers. These overlooked a restless Pacific Ocean which exploded into plumes of white spray every few moments. In the center of it all was an almost unbelievable sight—a slender medieval tower, one solitary turret, looking for all the world like part of a historic European castle.

The sound of the tide, the scuttling of crabs, and the cry of gulls filled the air with music. Beyond the tower was a rough mosaic of gray stone and sea. Tide pools gleamed in the cloudy light. A lone fisherman on a high rock braved the turbulent breakers.

Ah, but the tower! Something about it beckoned Betty. As she tried to run toward it, a wave broke across her path. She retreated, but not before both legs were soaked. In an instant, the saltwater attacked dozens of sores on her legs, ankles, and feet, setting them afire with pain. She was nauseated by the intense hurt and sank onto the sand.

"What happened?" At the sight of her daughter's sudden collapse, Lucilla's voice was sharp with alarm.

"Oh, it's okay." Betty's answer was a little shaky as she pulled herself to her feet, lightheaded. "The salt just hurts at first, that's all." It was true. Minutes later the burning passed, fading into a comfortable warmth. Later on, when the water splashed against her legs again, there was no pain at all.

Betty left Lucilla perched on a rock, gazing westward, and again ran wildly toward the tower. When she reached it, she clambered up the three stone steps that led to its weatherbeaten wood door. Predictably, the entry was securely locked from inside. Only slightly disappointed, she returned to Lucilla.

"What do you think it's for, Mother?" Betty was transfixed. "It's like something out of a fairy tale!"

"Well," Lucilla said dryly, "I doubt if there's a fairy tale involved. I imagine it's just a stairway to one of the houses on Victoria Drive. Instead of having the stairs outside like all the others, they've just enclosed them in a tower."

"Who do you think owns it?"

"How would I know? I don't know a thing about it."

Her tone dismissed Betty. Lucilla wanted to think her own thoughts.

What a wonder, being almost alone on that magnificent beach. As the sun broke through the fog, it spangled the water with light and wove rainbows into the sea spray. Seeing no one around but Lucilla and the fisherman, Betty pulled off her sweatshirt. Her bathing suit top allowed the sun to touch the rough skin on her neck and shoulders. Experience had taught her that sunburns are far less unsightly than rashes. She would be blistered by nightfall, and no one would know about her eczema.

God, I love this place. Gratitude turned her eyes beyond the scurrying remnants of fog. All at once there was an exhilaration inside her, some sense of elation she couldn't identify. *You know, it's a miracle I lived to see it. Sometimes I wonder why I'm still alive.*

To Betty, the ocean seemed vibrantly alive, too. Broad and vast and beyond comprehension, it was the closest thing to God she had ever seen. It was always there. It was immensely powerful. And beautiful—it was so beautiful.

"Mother, I think if the ocean was a woman, and if God was a man, they'd be lovers."

Lucilla was horrified. "Don't be sacrilegious, Betty," she snapped. "How dare you say such a thing?"

Fighting back tears, Betty quietly asked, "What do you mean?"

"I mean that you have some Christian responsibilities to fulfill, and sitting around daydreaming about God isn't one of them. You just build your foundation on good, sound doctrine, study the Bible, and keep yourself unstained by the world. That's all you need to know." Her voice rose as she continued. "And don't be sentimental about God. That kind of thing makes me sick."

Her outburst complete, Lucilla's sober eyes settled back on the western horizon.

Remind me not to mention that again. Anyway China's over there. She's probably feeling bad about not being a missionary in China. Betty recalled some past conversation with Lucilla about a mysterious "call" to the Orient, a call which had apparently been thwarted by her marriage to Harold.

She studied her mother's stern, bespectacled profile. *Too bad she never made it. She'd fit right in with the others.*

Moments later Lucilla got up, brushed off the back of her skirt, and looked at her watch. "Let's go. It's lunchtime."

Betty slowly made her way back to the tower, and rubbed her hand against it softly. "I'll be back," she whispered.

Just before she rounded the rocky point, she stole one last look. From that perspective she could see part of the French country house to which the tower belonged. A brand new dream dawned in her imagination.

Someday I am going to marry the man who lives in that house. I'll have a shiny golden bathing suit and a gold lamé robe. I'll sweep down the stairs, throw open the tower door, and walk along this beach as if I owned it.

She turned toward the stairs, smiling as she went.

Someday I'll be beautiful.

And someday the tower at Victoria Beach will be mine.

3

Sunday was a scorcher, and the air inside the Bethany Baptist sanctuary was stifling. Flies droned, old ladies fanned themselves with church bulletins, and Betty played "Almost Persuaded" on the piano as unobtrusively as possible. Right before her eyes, a near miracle was taking place.

Jerry Baldwin, who had steadfastly refused to acknowledge the existence of God for the past eighteen years, was standing with his handsome head bowed right in front of Bill Klienert. He had confidently stepped from the organ bench to the altar as soon as Bill's words gave him opportunity. Sweat glistening on his brow, Jerry was making what Baptists call "a public profession of faith."

Betty could see everyone in the building from her vantage point. At least three high school girls were weeping silently in their respective pews. Most notably, Brenda Williams sat alone, sobbing uncontrollably.

He knew she'd break up with him if he didn't get himself saved. Betty didn't mean to be cynical, but facts were facts.

For weeks, Bill Klienert had been reminding his Baptist Youth Fellowship members to limit their dating relationships to Christian believers. In the meantime, Brenda and Jerry had been frantically necking in vacant Sunday school rooms every time

Bill's back was turned. Beyond her adolescent passion, however, the pretty sixteen-year-old Brenda was developing a sincere desire for spiritual virtue.

The handwriting was on the wall. In his present infidel state, Jerry's days with Brenda were numbered. Surely this peril had not escaped his attention.

Up until today, Betty's love for Jerry had not diminished. She was leaving for college in two weeks, and Jerry was a sort of transportable dream. Since her entire relationship with him was sheer fantasy, it didn't matter if he cared about another girl or not. Nothing could tarnish her shining, imaginary moments with him.

During Bill Klienert's twenty-minute sermon that evening, Betty had been scrutinizing the congregation, intrigued by their indolence. The youth pastor was preaching about spiritual commitment. "What in your life prevents *you*," he gestured theatrically, "from giving the controls to God?"

The rustle of bulletins, a cough, and a sneeze were the only responses to his question. That is, except for an inaudible whisper in Betty Fuller's mind.

"Jerry Baldwin."

Betty squirmed uncomfortably in her seat. *Come on, God. Don't I even have the right to dream?*

She scratched her neck, then her arm. She looked around, trying to distract herself.

"Give Jerry to Me."

Leave me alone.

"What have you got to lose?"

By now Betty was thoroughly engrossed in some sort of inner argument. Was it with the Almighty? If so, as might have been predicted, He appeared to have the upper hand.

"What do you have to lose by giving Me your dreams? None of them ever come true anyway."

In less than thirty seconds, Betty inventoried her assets and liabilities.

The Almighty was, of course, quite right.

Well, if You think You can do better, go ahead.

Lucilla would not have approved of Betty's response. But, surprisingly, it was followed by waves of warmth that swept across her face, flooding her eyes with unexpected tears.

Look, God, You know I can't look any worse, so that's no problem. Just don't send me to Africa, okay? And, someday, please—let somebody love me.

As she left the sanctuary, a cluster of female admirers surrounded Jerry, smiling through their tears, welcoming him into the Kingdom of Heaven.

Betty walked alone to the car, leaving Jerry to Brenda and all the others. Who had she been arguing with in there, anyway? Was it really God? Had she just made some sort of a serious decision?

Now I'm really in for it. She shuddered as she started the engine, steeling herself for the worst.

Then curiously, in spite of everything, she began to laugh. "One of these days, I'm going to have to quit talking to myself!" she said aloud, burning a little rubber in the church driveway as she drove off.

"Mother! I've got a date! Can you believe it?" Betty had placed an urgent collect call to Lucilla from the pay phone at the Los Angeles Bible College girls' dormitory.

"Betty, that's wonderful! Who's it with?"

"Rick Remington. You know, the blond guy I told you about? He's in my Old Testament class."

"The Pentecostal?"

"Yeah, Pentecostal or Nazarene or something. Anyway, he's taking me to the Glen Oaks football game on Friday night, so you and Daddy don't have to pick me up at the dorm. He'll bring me home. Okay?"

Lucilla's voice disclosed genuine pleasure at the news. Fully aware that her eighteen-year-old daughter had never been out with a young man, she had periodically tried to warn Betty that with her skin problems she might not be all that appealing to boys. But now the long-awaited breakthrough had occurred. She sighed with relief. It was about time.

On Friday, Betty pushed her red cafeteria tray along the lunch line without selecting a single thing except a yeast roll and four pats of butter. She filled a cup with the mud-colored, hot liquid that spewed from the coffee maker spout. *I hope this stuff doesn't kill me.* She scowled at the suspicious-looking brew.

After generously diluting it with cream and sugar, she tried to wash the yeast roll down her throat. Butter or no butter, it was impossible. Betty sighed and shook her head. *I'm too full of butterflies for anything else to fit inside.*

The hands of the clock seemed motionless. Once her last class was over, she scurried up the stairs to the top floor, ignoring the elevator. There, safe in her tiny, drab room, she spent the afternoon pressing her clothes, perfecting her makeup, and staring out the window in a euphoric daze.

Los Angeles Bible College was situated right in the heart of L.A.'s urban center. The campus was self-contained in a run-down, thirteen-story building. Men's and women's dormitory floors were carefully separated by four levels of classrooms that were strategically locked every night. As one might have imagined, there were no coeducational visitation rights. Residents did share their quarters, however, with countless cockroaches and an occasional displaced rat.

None of these peculiarities disturbed Betty Fuller in the least. Whatever the surroundings, she was no longer living at 1715 Twelfth Avenue, Glen Oaks. Her new-found autonomy, however slight, caused her to count her blessings.

Betty's window overlooked crowded streets, noisy with traffic, and she could watch shoppers come and go from Broadway. An assortment of hotels, travel agencies, flower stalls, pharmacies, and coffee shops lined the busy sidewalks. Downtown Los Angeles throbbed with life, and she drew energy from it.

By now shadows were stretching themselves from one building to the next. Soon Rick would ring the phone in the hall, asking if she were ready to come downstairs. She checked her hair—again—sprayed it lavishly and smeared her hands with one final coat of baby cream.

Although her skin condition hadn't improved since her arrival at college, her disposition had been transformed. Some unprecedented zest for life had filled her with glee, which at times burst forth into noisy gales of laughter. Sedate students and dormitory authorities watched her with suspicion. But a light-hearted group of new friends shared her love of music, humor, and conversation, kindly tolerating her skin condition as well as her overenthusiasm.

She had met Rick in her Old Testament class where they sat side by side. He was a strong-featured young man in his early twenties. Far more mature than Betty, he had a good sense of humor and usually chuckled at her whispered commentary about their absurdly stuffy professor. After class one day Betty discovered that Rick had graduated from Lorenzo High School, the archrival football nemesis that battered Betty's alma mater every autumn.

As might have been expected, another infatuation took root. Day after day Betty sat alone in her dorm room, singing along with the love songs on the radio, longing for Rick.

Then the unthinkable happened.

"Listen, Betty, why don't we try to make it to the Lorenzo-Glen Oaks game together?" he'd suggested casually one morning.

She stared at him in disbelief. "You mean . . ."

"Sure. We'll go out to eat first and then go to the game." He misread the astonishment on her face for uncertainty. "If you want to, of course."

"That sounds like fun," she smiled, as coolly as possible.

I think I'm going to faint.

"I'm pretty sure the game's on the twenty-seventh, but I'll let you know on Monday. Anyway, have a good weekend."

Now, at long last, the twenty-seventh of September had faded into evening, the phone had rung, and Betty was greeting Rick in the downstairs lobby.

If she could have seen herself as she climbed into his black Volkswagen, she would have been mildly relieved. She looked unusually good. Happiness was good medicine. If not a cure-all, it had a distinctly positive effect on her appearance.

Half an hour later, seated at a small wooden table, Betty managed to swallow two narrow slices of mushroom-and-black-olive pizza.

At least he won't think I eat too much. I'd probably inhale the whole thing if he wasn't here.

After a final sip of Coke, she excused herself and located the ladies room. There she replaced her lipstick, touched up her makeup, and nervously rubbed more baby cream on her hands.

When the pair arrived at the football stadium, Betty walked proudly toward the stands with Rick at her side. As always, the schools' marching bands competed, each playing more raucously than the other. Cheerleaders hoarsely led the student sections in shouts of encouragement. The pep rally chants were still familiar to Betty's ears. But that night she felt like an altogether different person from the sad-eyed girl who had regularly accompanied Harold P. Fuller to the stadium.

She and Rick had agreed to sit on the Lorenzo side during the first half of play and to move over to the Glen Oaks side during the third and fourth quarters. As usual, Glen Oaks suffered a humiliating loss. But nothing could disturb Betty's bliss. A couple of people remembered her. "Betty Fuller?" one girl smiled, "Is that you? I didn't recognize you. You look so . . . different."

Days before Betty had sold a prize possession, her beloved *Complete Book of Marvels,* by Richard Halliburton. It had netted her twelve dollars at a used bookstore. With that small fortune, she'd bought herself a pair of $7.99 shoes, delicate off-white pumps that Lucilla would have considered highly impractical.

Next, she had borrowed a stylish pink skirt and sweater from

Sharon, a new school friend. Underneath she wore her own long-sleeved shirt, praying that she wouldn't ruin anything with blood or baby cream.

The final result was better than she had dared to hope. The sweater and skirt suited her. Pink flattered her. And her usually tense face was softened with smiles.

She glanced at Rick. *Well, so far so good. He doesn't seem too miserable.* She'd had no preconceived notions about the evening, because she'd had no idea what to expect. Unless Rick had simply vanished into the warm September night, she couldn't have been disappointed.

And in actuality the two really did have a delightful time. Rick seemed to enjoy himself thoroughly. Betty's fondest wish was that he might hold her hand—just for a moment. But considering the roughness of her fingers and the stickiness of the baby cream, it was just as well he hadn't.

At around 10:30 Rick drove his VW up Twelfth Avenue, pulled into the driveway, and walked Betty to her door. "Well, sorry Betty, but my guys won! Too bad. Maybe next year for poor old Glen Oaks."

Leaning over, he kissed her cheek very gently. "I think the world of you, Betty."

She stared at him in bewilderment.

He was unable to interpret the expression on her face. "Did I do something wrong?"

"No! No . . . it's just that . . . well, no one ever kissed me before. That's all."

He put his arms around her, hugged her warmly, and left without saying another word.

Betty Fuller might have been in love before. But she had always been, "The Great Pretender." Rick was real, and he had just given her a real kiss. A hasty shower scalded away her tension. Once in bed, she hardly slept all night. She relived the wonderful evening over and over again.

41

He can't really like me . . .

She tried to second-guess his motives. Why would he take her out if he didn't like her? But how could he possibly like her? What did he mean when he said, "I think the world of you"? Was that anything like "I love you"? Would he ever take her out again?

Days passed into weeks. Their friendly classroom exchanges continued, but Betty fought a growing sense of disappointment. Although he was always warm and jovial, Rick never suggested another date. Then one day he lightheartedly grabbed her arm as he passed her in a hallway.

"Let's skip chapel and go over to the Pig and Whistle for some pie. I'm not really interested in looking at a model of the Old Testament Hebrew tabernacle, are you?"

"Are you kidding? I've got one in my garage, and worse yet I helped build it. Let's go for the pie!"

She reveled in his company as they walked the three blocks to the café. Rick was a genuinely nice young man. Betty knew she wanted more attention from him than he was willing or able to give, and at the moment she was satisfied just to be with him.

They settled into a brown vinyl booth. "Now, Betty, pardon my curiosity, but why on earth do you have a model of the Hebrew tabernacle in your garage?"

Betty giggled. "Oh, Mother's a Bible teacher . . . you know."

"What church did you say you go to?"

"Bethany Baptist in Harvest Hills. Oh, by the way, my mother hates Pentecostals."

Rick laughed loudly. "Why?"

"Oh, she thinks speaking in tongues is from the pit of hell, and that people can't lose their salvation, whether they want to or not!"

They began to discuss the theology that lay beneath those issues. Lighthearted chatter was quickly transformed into a very serious dialogue. Betty went back to the dormitory understanding an unfamiliar point of view. She savored a growing sense of discovery.

It wasn't so much the subject matter that intrigued her, it was the resultant broadening of her mind. She liked to think, to compare ideas, to discuss possibilities. As she talked to Rick, she felt that some mysterious, unseen curtains were being drawn open. Light was streaming in from all directions.

On the way back, Rick insisted on stopping and buying two books. Before they parted, he presented them to Betty. One was a collection of writings by Charles Wesley. The other was a history of the Azuza Street Revival, a Pentecostal awakening that had taken place in Southern California in 1906.

Betty was overjoyed. He obviously cared about her, or he wouldn't have spent the money on the books. So what if he hadn't asked her to go out with him on another formal date? He didn't have to buy her pie and books unless he wanted to!

She caressed the books, rereading their covers, anxious to delve inside. Perhaps in understanding their content, she would be brought closer to the young man she cherished. She felt as if she were taking a small part of him home with her.

That weekend, Lucilla asked her about Rick.

"Oh, yeah, we went out for pie once this week." Her initial answer would have been quite sufficient, but enthusiasm caused her to broach a forbidden subject. She should have known better.

"You know, Mother, maybe Pentecostals aren't quite as bad as you've always thought. When Rick and I were talking, he told me some really interesting things about what they believe."

Lucilla's eyes narrowed dangerously. "Like what?" The words shot out of her mouth like bullets.

"Oh, he just explained some things to me, that's all. Nothing, really." Betty fled the room, hoping to leave behind the bitter animosity that had suddenly chilled the air.

Oh boy, I haven't heard the last of that one.

Silence reigned. The subject was closed for the remainder of the weekend, but Lucilla and Harold were both curt with their daughter, speaking to her only when they had to. She could hear them talking late into the night. Their angry tone was disturbing, muffled though it was by the bedroom walls.

The matter of Pentecostalism was exceptionally infuriating to the Fullers. And now their own daughter was privately questioning their biblical doctrines. How dare she? As far as they were concerned, her inquiry amounted to a personal insult.

Betty sighed, trying to tune in the radio, unable to find a song that excited her. *Rick cares about me. That's all that matters now. He thinks the world of me. He said he did. Who cares what they think?*

It wasn't until she unpacked her belongings in the dorm Sunday night that Betty realized that she had made a lamentable mistake. She had left behind the two books Rick had bought her. A sinking feeling made her momentarily dizzy. She scratched her arm unconsciously and soon found herself taking an unscheduled shower.

They are going to kill me . . .

She smiled a little at the thought of Lucilla's face, scanning the book jackets, reading the pro-Pentecostal copy that promoted their contents.

Still, Rick's friendship shielded her from the raw fear she might have normally felt. She hated to displease her parents, and would have never done so intentionally. But Rick cared about her. She was never quite sure whether Harold and Lucilla did or not.

By morning, her skin was a sight to behold. The areas that were normally red and scaly were further marred by angry scabs, evidence of frenzied nighttime scratching. She awoke with blood under her fingernails, her hair stuck to sores on both ears.

She worked desperately to cover it all up, but it was no use. Should she skip Old Testament? She couldn't bear the thought of Rick seeing her. Could she bear the thought of not seeing Rick? She went.

After class, he called her aside. "Betty, there's something I want to talk to you about."

She smiled joyfully into his eyes. Was he about to ask her out again?

Sensing that his words might hurt her, he endeavored to say them kindly. "Betty, this weekend I got engaged to a girl who goes to my church. Her name is Cheryl, and I want you to meet her. I know you'll love her—the two of you are a lot alike."

"Oh."

That's really wonderful, Rick.

The blow was so intense that it physically hurt. As his words struck her soul, she was rendered almost breathless. What could she say? The pause was growing far too long, but no gracious words emerged from her paralyzed brain.

"Betty, you don't look like you feel well today." He studied her closely. Rick was obviously unsure how to help the girl. He was genuinely concerned about her physical plight while unaware of the devastation that had taken place in her heart. "I'm worried about your skin problem. It looks like it's gotten a little worse."

Betty nodded.

"Do you have a doctor, Betty?"

Another nod. By now she was fighting tears.

"Here," Rick emptied his pocket change into her hand. "I want you to call your doctor and see if you can get an appointment. You don't want to let that stuff get the best of you."

Still clutching a quarter, two dimes, and a nickel, somehow she found her way back to her room. A relentless tide of tears overwhelmed her, surging from some deep harbor of pain. She cried until her eyes could hardly open. She cried herself to sleep, drenched in sweat, exhausted and without hope.

Hours later, she stirred. It was dark outside. Someone was pounding on the door. She glanced at the clock, immediately remembering her loss. "What is it?" Her voice was hoarse.

"Your father is downstairs, Betty," her friend Sharon's voice sounded concerned. "He wants to talk to you. To tell you the truth, he doesn't look very happy."

Daddy? He's supposed to be staying at work this week. What in the world is he doing here?

She quickly changed into a fresh dress, brushed her hair and rushed to the downstairs lounge. It was empty except for the menacing presence of Harold P. Fuller. He was erectly seated on the couch, his face florid with anger, his eyes cold as steel.

She sat down.

"Hi, Daddy! What are you doing here?"

"What do you think I'm doing here?" He pulled the two books out of his lap and threw them at her. One of the dustcovers ripped as it fell off the couch and landed on the floor.

Horror seized Betty. Her father had been angry before, but never like this.

"Your mother has not slept a wink for three nights because of you. You think you are so smart, don't you? Coming home from college with your 'new ideas.' Everything your mother has believed in, everything she has sacrificed to teach you, everything that she knows to be right before the Lord, you have rejected. You've turned your back on our doctrine, and as far as I'm concerned you've turned your back on us."

Betty was hardly able to think. Her voice was quiet, plaintive. "Daddy, I haven't turned my back on anything. I'm just trying to learn to think for myself."

"You aren't thinking for yourself at all. You're letting some wet-behind-the-ears Pentecostal boyfriend do your thinking for you. I swear to you, Elisabeth, I would rather he had raped you! Better that, than for him to violate your beliefs with his damnable heresies!"

"Daddy, how can you say that . . . ?"

"You have broken your mother's heart. I would rather you had been raped!"

Harold stood up and headed for the door.

"Daddy, wait, please . . ."

"Shut up. I don't want to hear another word from you until you've apologized to your mother."

With that, he was gone.

No one loves me. No one. Not one person in the whole world. No one ever has. No one ever will.

She found her way to the phone and called Lucilla collect. "Mother? Mother . . . I'm sorry. Whatever you say or think is fine . . . I don't want to fight with you . . . I know I'm a disappointment to you. I know. I don't mean to be.

"I'll try to be a better daughter. Please forgive me."

She hung up, took a blistering shower, and went to bed. It was three days before she was well enough to return to class.

"Sharon, what kind of perfume is that?" Betty sniffed the air. "Why do you smell like incense?"

Sharon, a pixie-faced brunette, laughed in spite of herself. "Oh, I thought Woody would like it. He's so homesick for Africa, and I keep trying to do things to make him happy."

Woody was a dark-eyed, intense young man who had arrived in Los Angeles from Nairobi less than forty-eight hours before classes commenced in September. The eldest son of missionary parents, he had a dry wit, a crooked smile, and he hated America passionately. Moreover, to his eternal credit, he'd met Aunt Abigail in Kenya and had assured Betty that he couldn't believe they were related.

"What has perfume got to do with Africa, for heaven's sake?" Betty squinted at her friend suspiciously.

Sharon tried to look coy. She couldn't, however, resist the opportunity to provide even more fascinating information about herself and Woody. "Oh, you know, it's sort of a joke. There's this new perfume called 'Ambush.' I told Woody I bought it to bring out the wild animal in him."

Dear God. I think I'm going to be sick.

"Will you do me a big favor, Sharon? If the perfume works, spare me the details. Okay?"

Sharon was sitting on Betty's bed. The girls were supposed to be studying for an English literature exam, but *The Canterbury Tales* had been abandoned in favor of more contemporary subjects. "Isn't this your birthday, Betty? What are you doing to celebrate?"

"Oh, I don't know. I'm twenty-one today, so I guess I ought to go on a wild drinking binge now that I can do it legally."

"I wouldn't blame you. After a few months in this penitentiary, we all need a good stiff blast. Listen, Woody and I are going to a movie this afternoon. Why don't you come, too? We'll pay your way for your birthday present."

Movies were off-limits to all LABC students. However, those who felt the urge to re-establish their sense of personal freedom occasionally transgressed.

"What movie?"

"Well, it's about Africa . . ."

Betty groaned. Loudly.

"What movie, Sharon?"

"It's a real classic called *Zulu* . . ."

"Zulu? What's a Zulu?"

"Who knows? Woody's mostly interested in the scenery. Ever since he got here from Kenya, he's been trying to explain to me what Africa looks like. I swear, he's more in love with Kenya than he is with me. Anyway, we're going, so why don't you come too?"

"Sharon, just tell me one thing. What on earth is so great about Africa?"

"I don't know. I just love Woody, and Woody loves Africa. Who cares why?"

As *Zulu* flickered on the screen, Betty was unable to discern even the thread of a plot. Her experience with films was admittedly limited, but once the credits rolled she shook her head in disbelief. There had been African warriors with spears, silhouetted along hilltops. African warriors on the attack. African warriors spearing other African warriors. And, in conclusion, African warriors celebrating their gory success.

In the theater lobby, Sharon and Woody decided to go back in and see it again.

"You've got to be kidding! What for?"

"You obviously don't appreciate the subtleties of Africa's culture, romance, and natural environment," Woody said, half-joking.

"I'm getting out of here. Enough is enough!" Blinking at the welcome sunlight, Betty headed for the dorm.

So I'm twenty-one today, and what do I do to celebrate? Everyone else on earth has a party, or goes out to dinner, or has cake with some friends. But me? I go to some stupid B movie about a bunch of bloodthirsty savages. I can't stand it! I've got to do something . . .

She was walking past an inexpensive spaghetti house. Impulsively, she marched inside. It was late afternoon, and the place was nearly empty.

"One?" a waiter asked politely.

"Yes."

He led her through a darkened room with clusters of plastic grapes bedecking a white-lattice ceiling. Each table was covered with a red-checked oil cloth, and was lighted by a single white candle.

Betty sat down, ignored the menu, and nervously ordered. "I'd like a glass of wine, please."

"Red or white, miss?"

"Red, please."

The waiter vanished into the kitchen, and reemerged with the wine and a basket of Italian bread.

Mother wouldn't sleep for three more nights if she saw me doing this. Well too bad. I am hereby old enough to do anything I please. Harold and Lucilla were teetotalers and expected every Christian believer on the face of the earth to be the same. Betty smirked at the thought of poor Lucilla walking in and seeing her only daughter drinking wine—alone.

She picked up the glass, lazily admiring the wine's rich color, intensified by the candlelight behind it.

Well, God, since you changed water to wine as your first miracle, you don't mind me having a little myself, do you?

49

She started to taste it, then noticed the bread. She pinched off a small piece, placed it in her mouth, and took a sip of wine.

"Do it in remembrance of me." Although inaudible, the words could not have been more distinct.

Bread and wine. Of course! How could I have missed it?

Betty's immediate thought was of the dour communion services at Bethany Baptist Church. On the first Sunday of each month, following an abbreviated sermon, six somber-faced deacons carried jangling, silver-plated trays of grape juice and crackers up and down the sanctuary aisles. Once the congregation sang "When I Survey the Wondrous Cross," Rev. Turner always gravely quoted the words of Jesus, "This cup is the New Testament of My blood. Do this in remembrance of Me."

Sudden, spontaneous laughter swelled in Betty's throat as she looked at the hearty, fresh bread and the ruby-hued wine set before her. She felt an unexplainable rush of joy, a sense of anticipation. Trembling with excitement, she lifted her glass to an unseen companion.

Okay. Fine. I'll do this in remembrance of You.

She took another small sip and swallowed it. The warm sweetness lingered in her mouth.

4

The old stone tower reigned proudly over the Laguna sea-scape, a benevolent monarch. Betty, ever the loyal subject, sat blissfully watching the ocean, basking in the sun's unseasonable warmth. From time to time, she turned her attention to the tattered notepad that rested against her knees. She was rewriting a verse for the hundredth time, forever contemplating its nuances.

Out of the Rick Remington heartbreak of two years before, streams of poetry had spilled forth, scrawled across countless sheets of paper. Like a compassionate counselor, Betty's literary ruminations placed labels upon her myriad feelings. Searching for "the right words" seemed to quiet her turbulent reactions. Writing even vaguely foretold eventual companionship.

Someday, somewhere, someone would read her words. If she were eloquent enough, he would surely care more about her thoughts than her ugly, scabby skin.

The sea was tranquil, almost glassy. That March morning Betty had impulsively borrowed her friend Sharon's unsafe-at-any-speed Corvair and had driven it far too fast down the Santa Ana Freeway. She'd left downtown L.A. at 10:00 A.M., and had arrived at her destination just minutes before 11:00. The wild ride had exhilarated her, and now she was joyfully sitting all alone on

Victoria Beach. Shouldn't a poet have a special place for writing? And didn't this beach all but belong to her?

Her pen moved quickly, in bold strokes:

> What was God doing in all that eternity,
> Before He unlocked the embrace of night and day,
> And light rays fell like tears upon the sleeping earth?
> Did He, with grim and powerful stroke,
> Devise man's will, and thus foresee his doom . . .

Momentarily distracted from her primordial considerations, Betty recalled a conversation she'd had with her English literature professor just weeks before. He had condescendingly reviewed one of her compositions after class.

"Well, Betty, I can see that you've been reading John Donne."

"What do you mean?"

"Well, obviously, you've been trying to copy his style. That's perfectly clear."

Betty was genuinely perplexed. She valued originality more than quality. She was incapable of plagiarism. How could anyone question her personal style? "I don't think I've ever read John Donne's poetry . . ."

"Well, you must have forgotten, dear. The similarity is far too marked for coincidence." With that, her teacher had politely excused himself from the conversation.

That's why I hate reading all this junk! Miffed, Betty lugged her books out of the classroom. *If you don't read it, you're ignorant. If you do, everything you write sounds like it's somebody else's idea.*

Betty's distaste for school had been intensifying over three long years. Listening to hours of droning lecturers rendered her almost chronically sleepy. Zoology. History of Western civilization. Issues in contemporary philosophy. What on earth did any of these subjects have to do with her?

"Well, dear, those classes will help make you a well-rounded teacher," a spinsterly school counselor had promised her.

So who wants to be a teacher? The thought of instructing a classroom full of bored students made Betty feel almost ill. And her grade point average of 1.75 confirmed her disinterest. She'd had few career aspirations when she started college. She had even fewer now.

Literature was the one subject she had always somewhat enjoyed. But this year, her enthusiasm was countered by certain nagging questions. How, for example, could some second-rate professor at a small, mediocre college possibly know what Dostoyevsky was thinking when he wrote his novels? How dare he pretend to understand Flaubert's literary intentions? And why should a class full of Christian students need to be warned about the immoral conduct of fictional characters?

Well, no matter now.

Soothed by the ocean's pleasant, persistent whisper, Betty stood up, whisked away the sand from her plaid trousers, and approached the tower. She tried the door. As usual, it was locked tightly. Sitting thoughtfully on the top stone step, she cupped her chin in her hands.

Betty Fuller, college dropout.

A broad smile involuntarily spread across her face. No more classes to face. No more homework. No more threat of disgrace. Not many days before, in one mighty act of surrender, she had quit school. Having thoroughly and incontestably failed, once and for all, the worst was over.

Betty's educational demise had saddened Lucilla and Harold only slightly. The removed financial burden had sufficiently eased their pain. Meanwhile, Betty had managed to keep her own room in the downtown dorm, renting it from the school with an eye toward full-time work in Los Angeles. To everyone's satisfaction, Betty Fuller would not be returning to Glen Oaks, California. Instead, she would begin her job search on Monday.

Harold and Lucilla continued to bewilder her. Lucilla could hardly stomach Betty's poetry, pronouncing it "sentimental" and "superficial." But, for some unexplainable reason, Harold kept a collection of every poem his daughter wrote. He never revealed his responses, or commented about content. He simply filed the verses, one after another, in a manila folder.

Obsessed as she was with her writing, Betty had looked forward to one particular college class with great anticipation. The LABC catalogue had described Poetry 302 as "an elective, focusing on creative expression." It turned out, however, to be Betty's final undoing.

She first suspected trouble when she learned that her poetry professor was Gary Drake, the boys' P.E. coach. How could he possibly be capable of teaching both subjects well? The thin open-mindedness with which she faced that dilemma quickly vanished during the first week of class.

Each student was requested to submit an original poem. "Bring in something you're real proud of," Mr. Drake's eyes were a little too glittery, his smile a little too cheerful. "And don't put your name on it. We'll pass them around, read them to each other and then critique them. It'll be fun!"

Betty felt apprehensive. Fun? She didn't want anyone critiquing her favorite poems. How could that inspire creative expression? Nevertheless, she followed the instructions. Atop the stack of assorted rhymes and free verses, she placed an extraordinarily somber contribution.

Even Betty shuddered as she glanced over it. It began in tragedy and ended in abject hopelessness. *Well, that's the way I felt . . .* Betty stoically prepared herself for rejection.

It came in the form of Esther McGinty, a thickly bespectacled student with mousy brown hair and an annoyingly sweet voice. She began to read Betty Fuller's dismal verse in a sing-song timbre.

> Misty curtains of tears hang,
> Long-spent tears,
> And as the curtains move, sighs echo.
> Dreams lie dying, in a twilight of yesterdays,
> And sorrow sings her song over again,
> Over again. Over again . . .

Halfway through, Esther abruptly interrupted herself.

"You know," her face was serene, "I just can't read any more of this. And I feel I just *must* say something. It really isn't *right* for a Christian to experience this kind of depression. No one who trusts God could possibly feel this way. And," she paused, gathering her courage, her voice ominously serious, "not trusting God is . . . well, it's *sin!*"

Betty was seething. *Oh, bless your righteous little heart, Esther. I guess you and your God just can't cope with sad people. Is that the problem? Well, believe me, your day will come!*

Betty's final disenchantment with the class came just minutes later. It took a somewhat different form.

When the poems were passed around, she had received one written in a thin, spidery hand. One reading and she'd immediately hated it. For one thing it rhymed, sort of, and was warped by an unbearably uneven meter. But far worse, it described the moon as "a baseball in flight, streaking through the Creator's cosmic stadium . . ."

"This is a most unfortunate metaphor," she had stated uncompromisingly, hoping to correct the folly of the anonymous writer. "The moon is too beautiful, too magnificent, to be compared to a baseball! Besides the poem's meter is uneven, and the meaning is trite."

Within minutes, Betty had learned the identity of the poem's author. It belonged to Gary Drake, sports enthusiast cum poetry professor.

Within hours she had dropped the class, swearing never again to expose herself, or anyone else, to artistic humiliation.

Within a matter of days, late in the February of her junior year, Betty Fuller had forsaken, once and for all, the sacred halls of Los Angeles Bible College.

Now a gentle March sea breeze tangled her hair around her face as she happily scribbled her thoughts. In spite of everything, tomorrow was on the way, seeming more a friend than a stranger. Peacefully, Betty sat in the shadow of the tower.

She was awaiting an unimaginable wonder.

Cigarette smoke hung in blue clouds around the stifling room. Tense and sweaty, a dozen tall, thin young women in various stages of undress were either yanking off or pulling on fabulous, expensive clothes. Once fully garbed, each model breathlessly checked the chart that was taped to her mirror, assuring herself that she was wearing the right garments with the proper shoes and jewelry.

A quick drag on a cigarette. Makeup blotted with crumpled tissues. One last, nervous primp. From the prompter at the curtain came the cue. One by one they glided onto the stage, lovely and composed and perfect.

To the audience it appeared that the regal women on the runway were incapable of hurry. Rhythmic music accompanied their graceful strides and turns. As they continued their fluid movements, Dorothy Maines' New-York-accented voice described the trends that would impact women's clothing for the next six months.

While the show progressed smoothly, Betty Fuller was a frantic participant in the backstage madness. Weeks before, she had been hired by the May Company's downtown personnel office, assigned to the retail chain's corporate fashion office as a clerical worker. Today marked a major fashion show, and she had forsaken her desk for an hour to work as a "dresser" for one of the models.

Over the past few weeks, Betty had seen dozens of these fascinating women come and go, carrying their large portfolios, slouching their way into Irina Mandelay's office for interviews. She had studied them unabashedly, gazing over her typewriter in awe. Now, for today's show, she was assigned to Monique, a friendly, green-eyed model with red hair. Betty's job was to have each of Monique's changes ready, unbuttoned, unzipped, and ready to slip on. The proper shoes were to be laid out in order, and discarded garments moved out of the way, or hung up whenever possible.

"What's wrong with your hands?" Monique had asked before the show began.

"Oh, I have a skin disease called eczema. It's not contagious—don't worry!" Betty smiled shyly.

"That's what I thought. I used to have that when I was a kid," Monique flippantly commented, then continued to check her chart against the clothing that hung next to it. "I'm missing a pair of bone shoes. See if you can find them, Betty."

Betty rummaged around, finally locating the large shopping bag that had transported Monique's accessories into the auditorium. Sure enough, there was the missing footwear.

"Here are the shoes." Betty stared skeptically at Monique's flawless complexion and meticulously manicured hands. "How did you get rid of it?"

"Get rid of what?"

"Eczema. You said you had it when you were a kid. How'd you get rid of it?"

"Oh, I don't remember. I took some pills or something. Benadryl, I think. Anyway that was years ago. Have you ever been to a doctor?"

Betty looked at Monique blankly. *Been to a doctor? You've got to be kidding. What kind of idiot would look like this and not go to a doctor?*

"Doctors have never been much help."

Monique nodded and lit a cigarette. "Doctors are jerks. What do they care?"

At that moment Irina Mandelay's voice cut through the noise in the room. "Fifteen minutes, girls. Please keep the noise down and doublecheck your changes."

Irina had hired Betty, or at least had accepted her as an assigned worker from the personnel department typing pool. Her first reaction to the ragged-looking girl had been one of disbelief. Why couldn't the people in personnel just once find a fashion-minded employee for the fashion office? They seemed to go out of their way to locate the most ill-suited individuals in Los Angeles for the job.

But as the days passed, Betty's intelligence saved her. Compliant and submissive, she had quickly learned her duties. "But what can we do about her looks?" Irina had asked Dorothy Maines, the Corporate Fashion Director. "The skin problem is one thing. But those clothes. And that hair. And all the rest of it . . ."

Silver-coiffed Dorothy, impeccably bedecked and bejeweled, sniffed in disapproval. "I say she's hopeless. But you've always been one to bring home strays. I'll leave that problem in your capable hands."

Irina was Dorothy's assistant, and the two had worked together for years. Dorothy was a diehard career woman, self-absorbed through and through. She was aggressive, profane, and generally inconsiderate of everyone but Irina and her own eccentric twenty-year-old daughter.

Dorothy Maines was thoroughly hated throughout the May Company, particularly in the ready-to-wear clothing division, where her quarterly "Pink Sheet" commanded seasoned buyers to feature certain trend-setting items in their departments. The buyers always lost money on Dorothy's selections, but they had to bow to her judgments. Her policies were indisputable. She always got her way.

Irina, on the other hand, was a former model, a delicate blonde who had been quite a beauty in her day. Now, approaching fifty, she was happily married to Javier, a fine violinist, and enjoyed her job simply because she loved fashion. She spent her spare time entertaining her arty friends and creating colorful, abstract acrylic paintings.

The day after the big fashion show, Irina invited Betty to lunch. She took her across the street to Berliner's, an establishment long respected by May Company's upper-level management. Hoping to direct the conversation toward the subject of her personal appearance, she inquired about Betty's interests.

"Well . . ." Betty took a quick breath. "I do write poetry."

"Really?" Irina couldn't help but be interested. She was

hopelessly attracted to "creativity" in whatever form it came. "I'd love to see something you've written."

Like a proud mother bearing pictures of her children, Betty Fuller just happened to have five poems in her handbag. To her credit, they represented some of her better efforts. Irina was genuinely impressed.

"This is absolutely fascinating, Betty! Honestly, I mean it. I think you have a lot of talent." That is what Irina said. What Irina thought was slightly different.

I've got to get this girl redone and dressed decently before the month is out. There's more to her than meets the eye—thank God in heaven for that! She's got some potential, but the poor thing desperately needs repackaging.

"Why are you working here? What are your plans? Do you want to be a writer?"

"I am a writer." Betty was surprised by the sharpness in her own voice and tried to retrieve herself. "I don't know what the future holds . . ." She hesitated, faintly aware that the future was nearly as foreign a subject to her as Latin, or worse yet, Greek and Hebrew. "I just want to buy some clothes and rent an apartment. I don't know about the rest."

"Well, if you're planning to buy clothes, why don't we go shopping together sometime?" Irina's eyes were wide with innocence.

"I'd love to do that—if you have the time."

Several shopping trips followed. Under Irina's skillful tutelage, style replaced cuteness. Quality replaced quantity. A precision haircut was introduced. Softer, more striking makeup was applied. Contact lenses were fitted. The improvement in Betty's looks was remarkable.

"Well done, Irina Mandelay!" The woman applauded her own success. In the long run, however, it wasn't so much her guidance that transformed Betty. It was her example.

Irina was self-confident, but quietly so. She was not preoccupied with appearances, but knew very well that they opened necessary doors in the world. In that decade, other young women were following in the fashionable footsteps of Cheryl Tiegs. Not Betty. In her grateful eyes, Irina was more than fashionable. She was an original. Most important of all, she cared.

Meanwhile, Dorothy Maines rarely spoke to Betty. For one thing, she was seldom in the office. When she wasn't tormenting the corporate buyers, she was terrorizing the branch store managers. And when she wasn't "in the branches," as she called it, she was in New York or Europe, gathering information for a brand new season of fashion totalitarianism.

After one lengthy absence, Dorothy reappeared at the downtown store. Just as the day was ending, she stopped briefly at Betty's desk, abruptly scrutinizing her dress.

"I hate that color!"

Betty's eyes flooded with tears of shame before she could control them. "Sorry . . ." she stammered, certain that she must still be an embarrassment to the fashion office.

Dorothy looked at her sharply. "No! Don't apologize. I should be sorry. That was rude of me. Whether I hate pink or not, the fact of the matter is that you're looking far better than I ever thought you could. Now if you'd just stop writing that awful poetry, you might turn out to be all right after all."

The unkind woman's words of good will were unexpected. Betty treasured them.

At that moment Monique called. She had been cut from the May Company's models roster after the last show. "Why, Betty?" she asked in forlorn voice.

"I'll have Irina call you tomorrow, Monique. I don't know what happened," Betty lied. Monique had gained weight and was filling out her size eight pants far too well.

"We don't need any more size tens," Irina had sighed.

Poor Monique. Betty liked the pretty redhead and had never forgotten her casual comment about eczema. "Oh, I used to have that . . . ," Monique had said.

Life without eczema was something Betty could not visualize. Walking home along bustling sidewalks that evening, Betty was lost in thought. *What would it be like to say, "I used to have that . . . ?"*

Unexpectedly, a distinct phrase resounded in her mind.

"I want to heal your skin."

Fear rippled inside her. "Leave me alone," she muttered aloud.

"I want to heal your skin."

"I'm fine the way I am. Leave me alone. I can't deal with that kind of hope."

There were a few moments of silence. Betty was growing more and more miserable with every step. "Don't you see how unfair it is to make me think about being well? I've learned to live with this. I'm fine. Now leave me alone! I can't stand to think about it!"

It wasn't unusual to hear derelicts talking to themselves as they trudged along the L.A. streets. And the few people who noticed Betty's after-hours monologue assumed that she was either inebriated, emotionally disturbed, or simply cursing a business adversary in absentia. As for Betty, she was unaware of anybody but the debate raging in her mind.

She stalked through the dorm's front door, angrily pushed the elevator button, and soared toward her room. Safely inside she fell to her knees beside her bed. "Am I crazy or is that you, God?"

"I want to heal your skin."

She began to cry, softly and in utter confusion. Lucilla and Harold M. Fuller did not believe in miraculous healings, except, of course, on the mission field. Neither did they believe in voices from heaven. For that matter, Betty had some fairly strong doubts of her own. And yet . . .

She rushed out the door, grabbed the pay phone and called Lucilla. "Mother? Do you think God might want to heal my skin? I think He just told me so."

On her end of the line, in Glen Oaks, Lucilla closed her eyes, placed her forehead against the wall, and shook her head. "What makes you think that, Betty?"

"I was walking home from work, and I thought I heard Him say, 'I want to heal your skin.'"

"Betty, did you hear a voice?" Lucilla's strained tone betrayed her struggle for control. Betty was forever testing her patience. What next?

"No, Mother. I just heard some words inside my head."

There was a pause. A long one. Then Lucilla's voice broke through the silence in a final statement. "Well, I don't know what you heard, or *think* you heard. Just don't get your hopes up, Betty."

"Okay, Mother." Tears constricted her throat. "You're right. I won't."

She hung up and slowly went back to her room. She knelt beside the bed. The agony of hope had invaded her world. It was a far greater burden than eczema. Hot tears stung her face, smearing her makeup.

"God, what do you want from me?" she choked out the words between her sobs.

"I want to heal your skin."

"All right, well then do it!" Scrambling to her feet, Betty stormed around her room, ripping off her clothes, leaving a trail of disorder as she undressed. She took a scalding shower and smeared herself with baby cream. Before she went to bed she found herself thumbing through an abandoned literature textbook, searching for distraction. Part of a poem caught her eye.

> Oh world, thou choosest not the better part!
> It is not wisdom to be only wise,
> And on the inward vision close the eyes,
> But it is wisdom to believe the heart . . .

George Santayana? Great. He must have been hearing voices, too.

She stared at the words, then closed the book, firmly and in immense frustration.

She didn't sleep for hours.

Betty squirmed, seated uncomfortably on the paper-covered examination table. Lucilla was perched on a wobbly green stool. The two of them were giggling uncontrollably, nearly blinded by tears of laughter. In all seriousness, just moments before, Dr. Calvin Mendoza had explained just why a sterilized injection of Betty's urine would forever cure her eczema.

"You are, most assuredly, allergic to yourself, Elisabeth. And, you see, only your own urine is able to desensitize you to your own allergens. It is truly an extraordinary breakthrough for individuals like you!"

Dr. Mendoza had been scientifically clarifying his mysterious new medical procedure. Betty had fought off her mirth until the doctor left her in the room with a small specimen bottle and a handful of tissues.

"The restroom is over there," he'd said as he motioned toward a narrow door.

This was Betty's second attempt at "getting well" since her encounter with the persistent inner voice three weeks ago. Wryly recalling some age-old Sunday school lesson about Naaman's rather nasty case of Old Testament leprosy, she had determined that the only Jordan River she could possible plunge into seven times was the local medical community.

Her first encounter had involved Benadryl, Monique's medication. Dr. Petrowski had willingly prescribed the little pink-and-white capsules, commenting that they just might ease Betty's itching. Benadryl had enabled her to doze through a week of work, but her skin had remained unchanged. Now her dear old physician had suggested this remarkably unorthodox treatment. "You never know," had been his only comment.

Still laughing uncontrollably, Betty inexpertly filled the specimen bottle and handed it to Lucilla. "He can't be serious," Lucilla cackled, gingerly holding the container. In spite of herself, she was unable to find anything sobering in the situation.

Betty waited twenty-five minutes for the sterilization process to be completed.

She cringed during the injection.

Only Dr. Mendoza's financial statement eventually removed the last traces of humor from his avant-garde and thoroughly ineffective "cure."

Betty longed to give up after that. But the remembered voice still nagged at her mind, and unwelcome hope continued to flutter in her heart. *One more try.* She promised herself that she would willingly declare herself a heretical lunatic after the third attempt. *Seven may have been the magic number for Naaman, but three will have to do for me.*

She consulted with Dr. P. one last time. He scratched his head, puzzled by her perseverance. Hadn't she and her parents been through all this enough times before? What else could he suggest?

In the back of his mind he seemed to recall that a new dermatologist had just opened a practice in Harvest Hills. She was well respected by her colleagues because of two brilliantly researched articles she'd had published in reputable medical journals. He hadn't yet met her but had heard a couple of positive comments. And unless his memory was failing him, the research papers had been about atopic dermatitis.

"Go see Dr. Margaret Johnson," he instructed, writing her address and phone number on a prescription pad. "Like I said before, you never know . . ."

The first appointment Betty could get was three weeks away. She was a little disappointed, feeling desperate to conclude her strange odyssey. Never again would she be swept away by her own emotions. Never again would she pretend that Almighty God would bother to tell her anything. Never again . . .

The fact was, Betty's vows were half-hearted. The wretched allure of hope was still tormenting her. Until her final attempt at wellness was a total failure, she would be unable to abandon the quest.

"Irina, I hope you don't mind, but I'm going to have to go to another doctor a week from Friday. I thought I'd just leave work early since my appointment's at three in the afternoon." Betty looked sheepishly at her boss. "I'm still trying to get my skin cleared up."

"No, that's fine." Irina checked her calendar. "I can stick around here that afternoon. Dorothy will be in New York, and we should be pretty well caught up by then anyway. You know, Betty," she hesitated, "I'm not sure, but I think your skin is looking a little better already." Forever sensitive, Irina hoped not to wound the girl. "And you seem to be scratching less. Is it my imagination?"

Betty unbuttoned her left sleeve and pushed it up to her elbow. It was true. She had noticed herself that some clearing seemed to be taking place. "Isn't that typical? You want the doctor to see you at your worst and you start getting better the minute you make an appointment!"

"Well, don't complain, Betty."

"I know. I'm just kidding." In actual fact, Betty was rather baffled. With every passing day, new patches of clear skin had been appearing on her legs and arms. Her face was requiring less makeup. Why?

By the time Margaret Johnson greeted Betty and gently examined her naked body, the skin was only half as broken out as usual. "It's really good right now," Betty explained, almost apologetically.

"It looks bad enough to me! You must be very uncomfortable."

Betty laughed. "I guess you could call it that. Totally miserable might be a better choice of words."

With that, Dr. Johnson walked out of the room and confidently returned with a handful of small medicine tubes. "I'm going to prescribe three different creams for you, Betty. The first is for general use, on your trunk and limbs. Apply it like this."

She demonstrated that a small amount of the cream would cover a large area quite effectively. "The second one is for your face and neck. Don't use the other two there." She smoothed a little dab on Betty's cheeks and throat.

"That doesn't seem like much at all," Betty was listening intently, wanted desperately to cooperate, sensing the woman's expertise.

"Dr. Johnson, do . . . do you really think this will help?"

"Oh yes. You should be pretty well healed up in a week. Now for your hands . . ."

"I want to heal your skin."

Unexpectedly, the all-too-familiar words broke dramatically through the doctor's instructions. They broke through the shadowy doubts that clouded Betty's thoughts. They broke through twenty-two years of disfiguring disease. Betty began to shake, tremors rippling from deep inside. Joy beat wildly in her chest, and she caught her breath. She no longer vaguely hoped. She believed.

Somehow, she believed.

"In a week?"

"At the most. Come back a week from today and we'll see how you are doing. My, you're cold, aren't you? Put your clothes back on, and I'll write out the prescriptions in my office. Come on in when you're dressed."

By now Betty was fighting tears. Still zipping her dress, prescriptions in hand, she rushed out to meet Lucilla in the waiting room. She tried to report the doctor's words, but could barely make herself understood. "A week. Well in a week. She says I'll be well in a week."

Lucilla looked at her daughter blankly. She tried to respond. She wanted to remind Betty not to get her hopes up. She longed to say, "Wait and see." It was too late. The words simply could not be spoken.

Against everyone's better judgment, faith's brave, lively mustard seed had sprouted and broken through the dry, hard soil.

Betty Fuller's healing had begun.

5

Golden hair gleamed, rhinestones sparkled as twin spotlights traced Elisabeth's every movement. Pirouetting down the long runway, green chiffon swirled softly around her ankles. Elisabeth was lost somewhere in Chuck Mangione's "Chase the Clouds Away," and only one who knew her well could have detected the slight hesitation in her initial steps from backstage or the tension in her jaw. Her chin was slightly elevated, her expression aloof. Blue eyes impassively scanned the rapt audience, seeing no one.

This was not Betty Fuller's first fashion show. She had been filling in for absentee models almost continuously since her skin's dramatic healing several months before. Her height, her slender frame, and her familiarity with fashion and accessories made her a natural substitute for the unfortunate girls who were forever being disabled by "food poisoning" hours before an important show.

"You're doing a fantastic job!" Irina smiled proudly.

"Better yet, I'm free! I save the fashion office budget a cool $60 every time I fill in."

"You know, Betty . . . Elisabeth, I think I just might be hiring you if you didn't already work here. That's how well you're doing."

"Strange, isn't it?"

"I think it's wonderful!"

Irina had spent countless hours working with Betty, rehearsing her steps, her "Dior" turns, her posture, and her facial expressions. The change in the young woman's appearance and manner was almost unbelievable. Some of the other models began to call the fledgling mannequin "Elisabeth," a more fitting title for her new personage.

As for Elisabeth, she was overjoyed to enter another season of her life bearing a different name. "Betty Fuller" had not endowed her with particularly pleasant memories.

Backstage the usual madness had prevailed. No longer a lowly "dresser," Elisabeth was determined to remain well organized and never to miss a cue. What if she made some dreadful error and was suddenly transformed back into the awkward Betty of old? Illogical as it was, the threat seemed oddly real.

After stepping out of her sequined finale gown, she worked feverishly to pick up her scattered clothing. "I used to be a dresser," she smiled at the short, plump girl who attended her, anxious to let her know that they were equals.

"Well, if I looked like you, I sure wouldn't be doing this!" the girl snapped.

Feeling rebuked, Elisabeth wanted to explain. But she stopped herself, instantly aware that miracle stories aren't for everyone. Some human conditions are simply not cured overnight.

The truth was, Elisabeth's transition from unappealing to glamorous had been abrupt, with little time for contemplation or emotional readjustment. She still felt like Betty on the inside and harbored an overwhelming sense that she was deceiving everyone, garbed in some clever disguise.

Disturbing dreams reflected this dilemma. Nearly every night she found herself painfully diseased once again, raw and itching and miserable. Upon awakening, she would rush into the bathroom and stare at the mirror.

I'm fine! she'd remind herself, sighing with relief. Her eczema really had become only a terrible memory. And yet a nagging question remained—had she really been touched by a power beyond herself? The truth was, in her most secret thoughts, Elisabeth stifled fears that her healing had been some magnificent trick played out by her own subconscious mind. For obvious reasons, she most certainly didn't want to offend God with such humanistic skepticism. And besides, ever the poet, she preferred to believe in the miraculous.

Meanwhile, Lucilla and Harold watched their daughter's metamorphosis in amazement and agony. Her present course was leading her realms away from the narrow confines of their existence. Her job, wardrobe, and manner were just, well, downright worldly. What in heaven's name had happened?

"Just don't forget where you came from, Betty," Harold growled one Saturday afternoon as she visited their home. "You're conceited now, always looking in mirrors. Well just don't you forget . . ."

Forget? Be serious, old man. Conceited or not, I don't need you to remind me.

Elisabeth Fuller had long since moved out of the LABC dorm and into a tiny studio apartment in West Los Angeles. Although it was far more expensive than the squalid student quarters, she luxuriated in her privacy, coddled her plants, rearranged her rattan furnishings, and tore around town in the tiny convertible Fiat she had managed to acquire—against Harold's prudent advice.

Her social life was limited to lunches at work and an occasional evening with Woody and Sharon, who had finally gotten married. She hadn't found a church in the west side of town that appealed to her. As a matter of fact, she hadn't really looked for one. This distressed Lucilla immensely. Try though she might, the poor woman seemed unable to stop harping about it.

"Oh, you're absolutely right, Mother! Next week, I'll go for sure." Yet somehow Elisabeth never quite kept her word.

Unfortunately, although most church services are intended to furnish opportunities for worship, Elisabeth was only able to view them as social events. Any communion she'd ever had with the Almighty in a church environment seemed to have occurred in spite of the setting, not because of it.

No matter what the circumstances, during those emotionally chaotic days she felt tense in the face of new acquaintances. She did not want to burden people with her past. Yet, at the same time, she felt dishonest about not revealing to them who she "really was."

Men were singularly troublesome. Elisabeth was unable to justify the fact that *now* they found her attractive. *Now* they wanted her attention. Invariably when a spark of interest flickered, she sensed the sexual implications immediately. Moving stiffly, speaking icily, she found herself physically backing away. *You wouldn't have liked me before, so leave me alone!* The unspoken statement was more than commentary. It was an angry, inward scream.

The Rick Remington episode had scarred her, and she wasn't about to take a chance on further devastation. So it was that, quietly absorbed with work, poetry, and occasional journeys to Victoria Beach, Elisabeth's twenty-third year passed.

One Friday in May, Irina mentioned to Elisabeth that she was certainly welcome to come to her home for dinner on Saturday night. In spite of the years they had worked together, it was the first time such an invitation had been extended. "We're just having a casual evening—wine and cheese, a casserole, and a light dessert. I'd love to introduce you to some of my friends. You and your poetry will fit right in!"

Elisabeth was curious, flattered, and delighted. Besides, Lucilla had mentioned a potluck dinner at Bethany Baptist Church scheduled for that very same night. "Everyone wants to see you," she had cheerfully assured her reluctant daughter.

That's all I need. A church potluck. Isn't there a funeral somewhere we could go to instead?

Something about Bethany Baptist Church made Elisabeth feel squeamish, at best. Now Irina's timely invitation gave her a glorious out. "Oh, Mother, it's sort of a business dinner, you know."

"Will alcohol be served?" Lucilla's voice was sharp with irritation.

"I don't know, Mother." Betty lied. Then, frustrated with herself, she went on. "Besides, so what if it is? I don't think God is any more offended by one lousy glass of wine than He is by five helpings of dessert!"

The conversation ended abruptly and, needless to say, on a rather sour note. Harold's immense potbelly had become a standing joke among the Bethany regulars. And Lucilla, though less self-indulgent, was ceaselessly fighting her own unsuccessful battle with the bulge. Nevertheless, Elisabeth felt guilty, wishing she'd kept her mouth shut.

But it's true! she grumbled to herself, seeking to soothe her conscience. *They have so much food at those things it's sickening. And they think they have to eat it all because it's wrong to throw it out! No wonder they're all so fat!*

Mentally tuning out that unpleasant conversation, she turned up the radio. After zipping herself into a simple white dress and tying her hair back with some fresh flowers, she checked, then rechecked her makeup. Elisabeth Fuller was forever trying to satisfy her craving for visual perfection.

Moments later she was steering the speeding Fiat around Mulholland Drive's curves and onto the Pacific Coast Highway. She pulled sharply into a parking place near Irina's house.

I'm so glad she and Javier live in Malibu. The air feels like a breeze from heaven!

Distant waves whispered. Climbing out of the car Elisabeth noticed pale-hued oriental lanterns swaying softly along the front of the house and the tranquil melody of wind chimes. Unexpectedly self-conscious, she became aware of other arriving guests. She certainly looked her best—her dress was a beauty. Three new poems, carefully typed, were tucked into her purse. Nevertheless, a powerful tide of shyness overwhelmed her, almost forcing her back to the little sports car.

Then, all at once, she remembered the Bethany Baptist pot-luck. She visualized middle-aged couples gathering in the dreary church basement. She could all but smell greasy fried chicken and bland spaghetti. She could almost see the groaning tables, deco-rated with plastic flowers, laden with shimmering jell-o salads and oozing tamale pies.

Suddenly she caught sight of Betty Fuller entering the room several steps behind Lucilla and Harold. The girl looked gawky. She felt out of place. A smile was firmly fixed on her face, and she was subserviently bearing the Fuller family's compulsory boy-senberry pie.

A surge of near-panic brought Elisabeth back to the present. *Never again!* she vowed. Summoning all her courage, she tapped resolutely on Irina's door.

It opened to a candlelit room, teeming with strangers. She walked in smiling. Trembling. Hoping for the best.

Carlton Casey was nearly forty years old, a debonair man with a deep, distinctive voice. He was handsome in an unpretentious way, graying at the temples, with friendly brown eyes. His clothing reflected his love of the finer things—an impeccable English tweed suit, a monogrammed percale shirt, a foulard ascot at the throat. Smoke from his pipe curled around his head like a fragrant aura.

Carlton had been an actor during his early twenties, and was now edging his way toward international success as a television director. He hadn't yet won his first Emmy, but everyone agreed that he was rapidly moving in that direction. For the past six months he had been traveling extensively, and he had just re-turned to pioneer an innovative new musical series.

In the opinion of Carlton's friends and acquaintances, the lengthy trip had served him well. Rarely had any of them seen him so relaxed, so easygoing. Those who liked him least had to admit that he even seemed to have acquired a rudimentary sense of humor. All in all, he appeared to be a changed man. Irina watched as Carlton and Elisabeth carried on a prolonged and seemingly intense conversation in a quiet corner of the room. She was pleased to see her young protégé so well entertained.

Irina had always been reluctant to invite Elisabeth to her parties because of her objectionable LABC background. Once upon a time, Irina, along with Carlton and a couple of others there, had done their own time at a small religious school. She had never shared this information with Elisabeth, because she no longer believed a word of the school's staunch teachings. Neither she, nor any of the others there, would have appreciated a theological dissertation from the likes of Elisabeth Fuller.

It wasn't that the girl made a habit of promoting her religion. It was just the uncanny healing of her skin and her firm insistence that "God did it." No one was more pleased by the results than Irina. She just didn't want any unwelcome tension at her dinner party.

But now, by the sight of Carlton's expression, it was evident that Elisabeth was doing something right. Carlton was a sophisticated and sometimes difficult man. If she could keep his attention, she could impress anyone.

Elisabeth, in the meantime, was enjoying herself immensely. This gentleman was a far cry from the overheated young men who had been drawn toward her in recent months. There was no trace of sexuality in his attention. He truly seemed to care about what she thought and appeared to be sincerely interested in her comments. She had not felt pressed to explain her "transformation" to him, so intriguing was the present course of dialogue.

In actual fact, he was doing most of the talking anyway. Carlton was telling Betty about his travels, and she was enraptured. A strange longing for faraway places with strange-sounding names stirred within her as he described cities and villages, foods and marketplaces and landscapes.

He, in turn, found Elisabeth to be a dedicated listener and surprisingly well-read. She was a perfect match for him physically, fair-haired and striking. Her clothing, reflecting his friend Irina's influence, satisfied his craving for good taste.

Perhaps most important of all, at an appropriate point in the conversation, Elisabeth brought up her writing. Soon Carlton was reading the three poems she had cautiously pulled out of her purse.

To her wonder, he read them again and again.

"You are amazing . . ." he said softly. "All this glamour and beauty, why it's just a veneer, isn't it? How could anyone so young feel so deeply?"

Elisabeth was caught off guard. "I . . . I've been through some . . . changes." She giggled nervously. "I guess we're all more than we appear to be, aren't we?"

Carlton looked mildly startled. "What do you mean by that?"

"I mean, I guess, as the saying goes, we shouldn't judge a book by its cover."

When the subject of religion found its way into their dialogue, Elisabeth explained that, yes, she was a Christian believer, and no, she wasn't attending any particular church at the moment. To her surprise, she learned that this man actually was a churchgoer. And, of all places, he attended Bel Air Presbyterian.

Mother would certainly be relieved. Better yet, he's only had one glass of wine—so far, at least.

After an elegant dessert of raspberries and cream, Carlton asked Elisabeth if she would like to take a walk with him on the beach.

As they strolled along together, she was aware of his closeness, but in an unthreatening way. The old thoughts of *I wish he'd hold my hand*, never crossed her mind. This was different, somehow. And at that moment of her life, the difference was a comfort.

"Are you terribly involved on weekends, Elisabeth?"

"No, not really . . ."

"Why don't you meet me at church tomorrow? We'll go out to brunch afterward. There's a place on the beach not far from here I think you'll love. The eggs Benedict are marvelous!"

"Does church start at eleven?"

"Meet me in front at a quarter of eleven."

By now they were standing beside her car. His lips brushed her cheek almost imperceptibly as they said their good-byes.

Driving home, Elisabeth was mystified by her feelings. There was no great excitement, no mighty pounding in her heart as far as Carlton Casey was concerned. She was far more tantalized by his uniqueness than by anything else. He was so thoroughly unlike anyone she'd ever known, it was almost amusing.

Fine clothes. World travel. Television career. Pipe. And yet he went to Bel Air Presbyterian Church. He thought she was beautiful and glamorous. He liked—maybe even loved—her poetry.

The lure was irresistible.

Okay, Mother. I'll go to church tomorrow. Didn't I promise you I'd visit Bel Air Pres one of these days?

In spite of the evening's pleasant outcome, some unexplainable disturbance troubled Elisabeth. It felt like fear, but why should she be afraid? Although her skin was as healthy as could be, she took a scalding shower. It seemed, in some symbolic way, to dilute the confusion.

Well there's one sure thing about Carlton Casey. It would be a cold day in hell before you'll find him at a Bethany Baptist potluck!

Laughing out loud, she wondered what she should wear to church.

"Our pilot sees it first—the mile-wide, forest-lined Zambezi. In a moment more we catch sight of the towering curtain of vapor rising high above the water. Beyond this vapor-wall we see not a trace of the river—only the jungle, rolling on."

Elisabeth had just returned from a rare-book store in Westwood, triumphantly clutching a copy of Richard

Halliburton's *Book of Marvels*. It had taken months for the store to locate one—a green one. There was another edition, a red-and-blue one, that was easily available. Unfortunately, the editors had changed the text and tried to update it. Only the green *Book of Marvels* would do.

Halliburton had been an explorer in the 1920s and 1930s. Before his final adventure, when his Chinese junk tragically sank into the Pacific, he had written numerous books, but his *Book of Marvels* had been directed primarily toward children. Little Betty Fuller had spent many a lonely hour poring over its spellbinding pages, soaring on the wings of silvery aircraft, sailing distant seas, exploring lands beyond the realms of her wildest dreams.

She rushed through the door of her apartment, yanked the thick volume out of its bag and quickly flipped through the pages to the chapter about Victoria Falls in Africa. She knew very well it was ridiculous, but she had to see—could the full-page photo of the massive waterfall possibly be colored with a blue crayon? Wouldn't it be extraordinary if she'd actually bought back her own childhood copy?

She sighed. The photograph was strictly black and white.

Still, a heartfelt wrong had been made right. Once the Rick Remington love affair had come to its painful conclusion, Elisabeth had regretted her hasty bartering of that matchless book. Now, having listened for months to Carlton's travel stories, she'd been compelled to find another copy. After all, Halliburton had taught her everything she knew to date about world travel.

Excitement tingled in her as she read the familiar words.

"What a strange sight—Victoria Falls from the air! It seems to fall up, not down.

"Safely landed, we move on foot back toward the Smoke that Sounds. We can hear the roaring. Through the treetops we see the towers of mist rising to the skies . . ."

The phone interrupted her. It was Carlton.

"Why don't we drive up to the cottage and see if you think

you'll be comfortable there? It's small, but, really it's just so fabulous."

Carlton owned a tiny English country home, set in an ivy glade among the Hollywood Hills. Thus far, he'd never taken Elisabeth there. Last night, however, he'd suggested that they consider marriage.

"It would probably be a good idea," had been her down-to-earth response. In light of that, a trip to the cottage was in order.

It was in this very way that their relationship had evolved—nothing passionate, nothing emotionally risky. Ever the gentleman, Carlton had sought little more than a good-night kiss from Elisabeth. Perhaps he knew that chastity had been a matter of supreme importance at LABC, as well as holding a lofty place among the edicts of one Lucilla Fuller.

No matter. Limited as Elisabeth's experiences with tenderness had been, she was quite content.

Carlton settled her in the front seat of his vintage Jaguar. They wound around Laurel Canyon Boulevard, down several narrow lanes and finally parked in front of the little house.

Carlton lived in a lavish Brentwood apartment, but he treasured his "enchanted cottage" in the hills. Small though it was, he imagined that the two of them could settle there quite comfortably.

What better place to set the stage for "happily ever after"?

When the door opened, a waft of cool air caressed Elisabeth's face—it bore a pleasant musty smell that announced the presence of countless antiques. The entire abode was furnished with priceless English oak, circa 1750–1820. The oriental rugs, curtains, bedspread, couch, and chairs blended together in rich shadings of wine and blue. Imari china decorated the carved mantel pieces of both fireplaces, and exquisite blue-and-white Chinese urns graced the living room hearth. The bedroom floor was waxed brick, the living room, highly polished wood. It was a matchless jewel of a house, with a flower-garden view from every leaded window. Tudor on the outside, museum-perfect on the inside.

Elisabeth was speechless. This was a place to be dreamed about while thumbing through *Architectural Digest*. Could it be true that she would actually live here? She could hardly imagine herself as lady of the house.

Carlton bustled about, opening windows and chests, proudly displaying for her the finest of his antiques.

"The closet is a tad small, but then there is the armoire. Maybe we could find another . . ."

"Carlton, it's just wonderful. I really can't believe my eyes." If she said it once, she said it half a dozen times.

While they made their way back toward West Los Angeles, she impulsively remarked, "You know, Carlton, for some reason your cottage reminds me of a house I've always loved at Laguna Beach."

"Really? Where's that?"

"Have you ever heard of Victoria Beach? There's a house there with a sort of European-style tower . . ."

"Oh, yes, Le Tour."

"Le Tour? Is that the name of the house?"

"Yes, of course. That's James Novak's house. He's a friend of mine."

Elisabeth gasped, her head spinning with excitement. "Carlton, I've got to meet him. I really do. You see, I've gone to Victoria Beach since I was a little girl, and . . ."

Interrupting her explanation, Carlton laughed, a little too loudly. "James? Oh, don't worry. You'll meet James."

There was a momentary pause, while Carlton collected his thoughts. He laughed again, his eyes bright with some private mischief.

"Don't worry, Elisabeth. You will most certainly meet James Novack!"

Betty was paralyzed by a frenzy of itching. She dug at her arms with her nails and still the intense urge continued. Rushing to her nightstand, she found two combs, grabbed one in each hand, and desperately began to scrape at the skin on her forearms. Before she realized what she was doing, deep gashes appeared, beading heavily with blood.

Horrified, she ran to the sink and plunged her arms under the surging faucet. The pain was excruciating. The humiliation of such self-destruction was overwhelming. Watery blood was everywhere. Frantically, she reached for a towel.

"Oh, God, help . . ."

Elisabeth's own voice awakened her. Shaking with terror, she clicked on the lamp and examined her arms. They were clear.

Thank You. Thank You. Thank You.

Not many years ago it had really happened. Now it was only a hideous dream.

Squinting at the clock, she realized that it was barely 4:00 in the morning. Shivering, at last she fell asleep again.

She soon found herself marching down the aisle at Bethany Baptist Church, outrageously attired in a garish antebellum bridal gown, hoop skirt and all. At the altar stood Carlton.

She took one look at him, turned, and ran out of the church screaming.

In another instant she was fifteen years old again, weeping beside Grandma's bathtub. Bitter tears soaked the ugly green carpet.

Once more she awoke.

Only 5:00 A.M. This time sleep would not return. Her mind raced.

Two more days and she would be marrying Carlton Casey. There was a certain excitement implicit in the prospect of a new life. Nonetheless, she felt no particular sense of anticipation about actually being Carlton's wife. It just seemed like the appropriate thing to do.

Twinges of worry sent her tossing about in the bed, pulling out the blankets from the bottom. Sweaty and uneasy, she recalled the day she'd revealed her wedding plans to Irina.

"You and Carlton? Married?"

What had Irina's eyes reflected? And did her face grow momentarily pale, or had Elisabeth's eyes deceived her?

"What's wrong, Irina? I thought Carlton was your friend."

"Oh, nothing, nothing Bett . . . Elisabeth. Of course we're friends. And, of course, I couldn't be happier. It's just, oh I don't know. You seem so young and free. Are you sure you're ready to get married?"

Irina was rattling on far too fast, and Elisabeth realized that there was more to this conversation than she would ever hear. What was the right question to ask? And what might the answer be?

Then, of course, there had been the peculiar exchange with Lucilla and Harold just the day before. Lucilla, as usual, was acting like two different people. One was the happy mother of the bride. But the other seemed unlike her usual stern self. This Lucilla was a curiously pensive woman, bearing an unspoken worry.

"Betty, are you sure he's never been married before? He's nearly forty, isn't he?" Lucilla's eyes had been fixed on her stove, which she was frantically polishing with Jubilee.

"Mother, I'm absolutely sure. We have no secrets from each other. And I know how you feel about divorced people remarrying."

"He acts like a queer," Harold had barked from another room. He hadn't missed a word of their conversation.

"Harold!"

At times her husband's Marine Corps background disgusted Lucilla. This was clearly one of those times. "That's a fine thing to be saying about your daughter's husband-to-be!"

"I'm not saying he *is* one, Lucilla. It's just that some of these rich fourflushers act like queers. That's all."

The door slammed. Having made his statement, Harold headed for the hardware store.

Lucilla and Elisabeth had looked at each other and shrugged.

"If a man dresses well and doesn't like sports, Daddy thinks he's a queer. He always has, he always will."

"Well, just forget it, Betty. Carlton is going to be an important part of our family, and I promise we'll make it work."

"Mother, Carlton's a Christian. And you know that's the most important common ground in a marriage. To tell you the truth, he's more concerned about churchgoing than I am!"

Lucilla's nod of understanding had closed the subject. She was soon back to cleaning the kitchen with all her heart and soul and mind.

Now, a periwinkle dawn brightened the sky, and a thousand birds caroled outside Elisabeth's window. Wearily, she threw off her covers and sat on the side of her bed. She stared at her manicured hands, a two-carat diamond solitaire twinkling on her finger. She studied it absently.

Turning her eyes toward the window, she thought about the love songs she'd treasured just a handful of years before. She mourned some lost dream of wedding day magic. Then, unexpectedly her joyful football outing with Rick Remington came to mind.

I'd have had a heart attack if I'd married him. She laughed softly at the thought. So what? She was willing to give up her romantic fantasies for the rest of her life, just to enjoy Carlton's company and his fabulous Hollywood world. Imagination for reality—that was a fair trade, wasn't it?

Boy, talk about premarital jitters! Elisabeth pulled open her curtains with a vengeance. *No wonder there are so many divorces— people get all emotional and then make terrible mistakes. At least Carlton and I are good friends. This is the way mature people get married.*

Next evening Bel Air Presbyterian Church was ablaze with candles. A string quartet played softly, and a small vocal ensemble gathered in the choir section.

Elisabeth glanced at her father as they awaited the processional. He wore his usual inexpensive suit, starched white shirt, and plain navy blue tie. His jaw was set, his teeth clenched, his eyes blurry. He looked like he was about to get into a fight. She smiled at his nervousness.

"I love you, Daddy." The words were whispered only to him.

He patted her hand and nodded. Elisabeth was a vision in ivory lace and pearls. He had never seen her look so beautiful, or somehow, so vulnerable. Tears were dangerously close to spilling down his cheeks.

Soon the burly man and his pristine daughter were the center of attention. The choral ensemble breathed forth a wave of classical harmony, accompanied by flawless strings. The conductor was a veteran of the civic light opera. The music was superb.

Carlton had made all the wedding arrangements and had discreetly managed to pay for everything but the flowers. This was, on the surface, a benevolent gesture, since Lucilla and Harold had little money to spare. But, beyond that, Carlton wanted his wedding to make the right impression on a rather large number of people. Considering the quality of life most of them embraced, good perceptions didn't come cheaply.

Elisabeth had always wanted to carry a bouquet of lilacs at her wedding. But Lucilla loved orchids and had nearly burst with excitement, having located a vast orchid greenhouse with exceptionally low prices. Elisabeth had pretended to share her delight. Now she looked down at the fragile cymbidium orchids and was strangely pleased to be carrying them.

A lot of things I've said and done have made Mother's life miserable. Today, if orchids make her happy, I'm happy too.

After the private dinner party Carlton hosted at a fine French restaurant nearby, the two waved good-bye amidst a whirlwind of rice and sped off to San Diego for a weekend honeymoon at a friend's beach-front condominium. The television season was picking up, and Carlton didn't want to be away past Sunday. "We'll go to Europe when the hiatus comes," he promised. "And we'll stay in all the best places. You'll love Europe, Elisabeth."

The intimate moments they shared that night were Elisabeth's first. Carlton was, by nature, a gentleman and clearly not given to passion. As for her, she was more nervous than stimulated. The final moments of the experience found her abandoning her girlhood with more than a little sadness. Afterward, she lay sleepless and melancholy in her new white satin negligee, her groom dozing fitfully beside her.

Good grief. If that's all there is to it, I'm surprised people get into so much trouble.

Turning over, she brushed away a grain of rice that had fallen from her hair onto the pillow. Seeking happier thoughts, she imagined breakfast tomorrow and years to come in the Hollywood Hills cottage.

6

Like a jealous sentry keeping a watchful green eye on hoards of Southern California money, Bullock's Wilshire's art-deco tower soared in splendor above the traffic below. Fine automobiles came and went beneath the shadow of that familiar Los Angeles landmark, some chauffeured, some driven by well-bred women who were eternally grateful for the convenience of valet parking.

Bullock's Wilshire was the cream of the Wilshire District specialty stores—*the* place to shop. Past the heavy glass doors, beyond the marble cosmetic aisle, fashionable treasures were neatly arranged on counters and hung on t-stands. Nothing but the finest merchandise found its way into the grand old establishment that called its customers "patrons" and counted the city's wealthiest elite among them.

On the fifth floor was the models' room, adjacent to the president's office and the mauve-and-green Tea Room. Every morning, just past 9:00, several women arrived there, each opening the door with a brass key tied to a red ribbon.

This spring morning, Elisabeth Casey placed her key in the old lock, turned it until the door swung open, and crossed the plush carpet to her "place"—one of eight locations along a white-enameled vanity counter. It featured a drawer and a chair and was marked by an ancient mirror on which "Elisabeth" had been painted with scarlet Chanel nail polish. A window next to her overlooked Wilshire Boulevard and was cranked open to receive a warm Santa Ana breeze.

It was quiet in the big, airy room. Pairs of gold and silver evening shoes were hung on pegs, their soles covered with masking tape. A week-old bouquet of yellow roses wilted in a crystal vase on the center table. The racks that lined the walls were empty—it would be Elisabeth's job, along with the others, to go to two or three assigned departments, select six changes, and accessorize them with shoes, jewelry, scarves, hats, and handbags. Noon until 2:00, Monday through Saturday, the models worked a small runway and then chatted with business-men and society women who filled each table in the room. The Bullock's Wilshire Tea Room fashion show was a Wilshire district tradition.

Elisabeth looked around to see whose bags were already there. Julia. Leah. Carmen. Rebecca was always late. Elisabeth sank into her chair and studied her face for a moment. She noticed circles under her eyes and quickly opened her square makeup bag, rummaging for cover-up cream.

For about four months, Elisabeth had been employed by Bullock's Wilshire. She and Irina had tearfully parted just two weeks after her marriage to Carlton when, unexpectedly, Javier had been invited to join the London Symphony. Thrilled by the opportunity, and forever open to new adventures, the couple had leased their Malibu home and rented a flat near Chelsea.

"Will I ever see you again?" Elisabeth had mourned.

"Carlton will bring you to London, Elisabeth. We'll see each other before you know it!"

Life had seemed empty without Irina's company, and May Company no longer felt like home. Besides, although he'd never really said so, it had become increasingly evident that Carlton was a bit embarrassed by his wife's vocation.

"You look like a model, but you're really just a clerk. You model whenever they ask you to. Why don't you just *be* a model?"

Elisabeth had been flattered by his words. Maybe she could make it into photography modeling—"print work" as it was called in the business. *It'll be a lot more fun than walking up and down runways for the next ten years,* she had promised herself, trying to counteract her insecurities. Not quite convinced, she had nevertheless courageously approached a representative from the renowned Nina Blanchard Agency. Her worst fears confirmed, she had left the chrome-and-white office thoroughly deflated.

"Your nose is too prominent, darling." Between drags on a brown cigarette, the woman had eyed her with impenetrable disinterest. "You'll need to see a surgeon about that . . ."

My nose? It's always been just fine the way it is, thank you.

Fighting tears, gulping gray Hollywood air, she stalked back to her car. Mr. Murphy's kind words from years ago still floated through her mind, ". . . the prettiest little nose I've ever seen."

If my nose was good enough for Mr. Murphy, it's good enough for me!

After that bleak farewell to her faint hopes for cover-girl status, she made her way, nose and all, back to a more familiar environment. Bullock's Wilshire was "*the* place" to work as a model in Los Angeles. The flamboyant fashion director was oft quoted in the *L.A. Times* "View" section, and the best designers in America brought their collections there.

Still bruised from her Nina Blanchard episode, Elisabeth walked tentatively into Stephen Andre's posh "salon," as he liked to call it. Stephen was an middle-aged, elfin creature, decidedly gay, who possessed a wickedly funny sense of humor.

"Where did you get that fabulous vest?" she asked him, hoping to break the ice, admiring a bold tapestry waistcoat that seemed to float above his carefully pleated pants.

Stephen placed his hands on his hips and posed haughtily, "Does Macy's tell Gimbel's?" He tossed his head and giggled uproariously, the ice clearly broken.

What a flaming queen. He's more feminine than I am.

Once they got down to the business of her job interview, she'd really felt quite relaxed. Stephen asked her to try something on so he could see that, yes, she really was a size eight. "You'd be amazed at how some of these women *lie* about their size . . ." he sniffed in disgust.

Elisabeth zipped herself into a long, backless white gown and walking out of the dressing room spontaneously did a couple of Dior twirls for him.

"My heavens, Miss Elisabeth. You have such marvelous, golden skin," he exulted, studying her back. "Not a blemish."

"It's a miracle . . ." she wanted to tell him why. The story seemed outrageously inappropriate.

Convinced that she would fit right in with his other "girls" and without further ado, Steven Andre (or "Mr. Stephen," as he preferred to be called) hired Elisabeth Casey as a Bullock's Wilshire house model. At last she had officially become a professional.

Despite her initial elation, the job, like all jobs, became a bit mundane. This morning she felt particularly tired, maybe even a little depressed. The night before, a television taping had gone on into the wee hours, and she had stayed for the duration, expecting to eat out with Carlton after the wrap-up. As it turned out, he had gone somewhere with the producer and the art director. She had a bowl of cereal at home, feeling more than a little dejected.

Their marriage, just four months old by now, had settled into a pattern of activities that orbited around Carlton's production offices, NBC and ABC television studios, Bullock's Wilshire, a few fine restaurants, and church at Bel Air Presbyterian—when Carlton wasn't working. It was a comfortable life in that there were no financial pressures, few confrontations, and, for Elisabeth, no particularly demanding responsibilities.

During their first month, she had succumbed to but one frustrated outburst. "You never come home before midnight, Carlton, and when you are home, you don't say three words to me. What am I doing wrong?" Her question had been thoroughly sincere. In response, Carlton had coldly explained his marital philosophy to her, making one thing clear from the outset. "My work comes first!"

"You know, Elisabeth," he continued, "I remained unmarried for many years because I didn't think any woman could possibly cope with my career. Up until this . . . this little tantrum of yours, you seemed very different from the others. I certainly hope I wasn't wrong."

Elisabeth was sincerely sorry. What right did she have to expect her husband's undivided attention? He was a busy, important man, and she was fortunate to be his wife. All marriages weren't meant to be the same, and she was more than willing to make the necessary adjustments. Once that unpleasant scene was behind her, she felt fairly content as Carlton Casey's wife.

And in many ways the adjustments were well worth the benefits. Her low-pay, high-visibility modeling job brought her into a world of lavish glamour. Day after day, with her hair and makeup absolutely beyond reproach, she pirouetted beneath flattering lights, garbed in the most spectacular clothes imaginable, reaping countless compliments. Life had taken an extraordinary turn for the better. She could still remember tearfully making her way across the Glen Oaks High School cafeteria, hoping no one would notice.

How very far away poor old Betty Fuller seemed!

Besides, there was more to the intriguing scenario than pretty clothes. Working in the models' room had a certain similarity to a real-life television serial. With the exception of Elisabeth herself, every model in the room seemed to be in the midst of a captivating, dramatic story.

Julia, for example, had been a Vogue model in the 1950s. She was an elegantly structured British beauty, now silver-haired and in her late fifties. She had recently divorced Mel Frankel, an Academy-Award-winning film producer. He had left Julia for another woman, an actress whose name Julia would never reveal.

Recently, Mel had been coming over to Julia's home late at night, pleading for her company. Whenever and wherever he traveled, he still called her daily. Yet he continued to nurture a wildly mercuric romance with the actress, a relationship that he had no intention of ending.

At 11:45, the models' room phone rang. It was always Mel. He and Julia whispered for fifteen minutes until it was time for Leah to walk through the models' room door and into the Tea Room, beginning the show.

Leah was a wispy blonde with immense brown eyes. She was sought out by a seemingly endless stream of suitors—sadly, most of them were unhappily married. More than one irate wife had called Leah on the room phone, demanding explanations.

Leah wasn't really a home wrecker; the homes were invariably in shambles before she entered the picture. She was, in the minds of most men, what their wives were not. She was beautiful, slim, witty, independent, and a remarkable listener, her gentle eyes never leaving the face of the one who spoke to her.

To the continuous amazement of Elisabeth, who had hitherto firmly believed that all attractive women had their choice of male company, Leah was incredibly lonely. She had been through three devastating love affairs in the past two years and was as emotionally fragile as the fine, bone china cups she collected. Someday, somewhere, Leah and her perfect husband would sip coffee together in the house of their dreams.

A 1960s Miss Mexico, Carmen was usually the second model out. A dark-eyed temptress, she depicted herself as having "hot Latin blood," and her lifestyle did nothing to contradict that. When Elisabeth met her, she was co-habiting with a Korean War veteran who periodically shot holes in their living room ceiling with his pistol. Meanwhile, she was having an affair with the president of the store, Karl Goldfield, whose Pasadena blue-blood wife was, to hear him describe her, "a Frigidaire."

In the course of barely three years, Carmen and "Mr. G," as she affectionately called him, seemed to have played tennis and heaven knows what else at every luxury resort in North America. And, thanks to Carmen, everyone in the room wanted to work Fridays when Mr. G. faithfully sent champagne and dessert to the models' room—anonymously, of course.

There were several freelance models who didn't keep a regular schedule. Red-haired Dana, for example, was married to a linebacker for the Rams. She worked only Thursdays, lived a quiet life raising two children, and flew to football training camps and games for more than half the year.

Rebecca, a flamboyant black model, came in weekly with a new tale of lust and passion. "I lost my virginity last night," she would announce to her amazed friends, "all over again!"

Anne was in and out of her plastic surgeon's office and back and forth from New York. She was trying to make it in the print business. Whenever she worked, Anne displayed a different piece of jewelry, each a glittering gratuity from her famous actor-lover, a matinee idol who would never allow himself to be seen with her in public.

Only Elisabeth Casey seemed to be without a tale of woe or wonder. Dressed and made up for some leading lady's role, always ready with the right lines, Elisabeth was nevertheless waiting just off stage. She was nothing more than an innocent bystander, forever in the audience.

As she steered the white Jaguar onto the NBC lot, the guard at the gate smiled and waved at Elisabeth and nodded pleasantly to her two companions. He was a cheerful, round-faced man, always happy to see a pretty face.

Once inside the network facility, the three women made their way down the long, drab hallways toward the west side of the building, their high heels clicking against the tile floor. Inside Studio B, lights blazed with eye-aching intensity. Elisabeth, Leah, and Carmen were seated in the audience of Carlton Casey's

"Musical Showcase" television show. He had seen his dream show into reality that fall, and his efforts had been welcomed by rave reviews in the industry trade papers. "Small-screen genius!" *Daily Variety* had rejoiced. Surely this would bring forth the long-awaited Emmy.

"Take three!" said a disembodied voice, and for the third time Neil Diamond sang "Hello, My Friend, Hello," backed expertly by a live band.

Leah nudged Elisabeth, "See? I told you he was singing to you. Don't pretend you didn't notice!"

Elisabeth retained an inscrutable countenance, but her face burned. Yes, there seemed to be no doubt about it. The singer had almost certainly looked right into her eyes as he sang the familiar words, ". . . and I think about you all the time . . ."

It wasn't unusual for the three Bullock's Wilshire models to receive a prodigious amount of male attention. Wherever they went, at least one of them appealed to someone. But Neil Diamond? This was an altogether different matter.

To further complicate the situation, during the taping Carlton had barely spoken to his wife and her friends. Understandably, he was immersed in the show. He remained in the upstairs booth most of the evening, only emerging occasionally to talk to the production assistants or the art director. When Elisabeth had finally caught his attention with a tiny wave, he scowled at her.

She hoped the girls hadn't noticed, but of course they did. "What a bore!" Carmen muttered. "He's exactly like my ex-husband. He was in the business too, and was he ever married to his job!"

Leah, unfailingly polite, just shook her head slightly and smiled at Elisabeth. "Who needs him? Listen, kiddo, if you wanted to, you could spend the night with the King of Diamonds."

Elisabeth was veritably stunned by the entertainer's attention to her. Had he really been looking at her, or had the three of them imagined the whole thing?

There was a break in the taping, and Carmen suggested they leave—it was nearly 10:30. "I need my beauty sleep," she reminded them, primping in her compact mirror. Through take after take they had smiled and applauded, obedient to the prompter's commands. Drained of all genuine enthusiasm by now, they were more than happy to go.

The car was barely out of the parking lot when Leah asked ingenuously, "Elisabeth, what do you like best about Carlton? You two seem so opposite, and I'm always curious about what attracts people to each other."

Elisabeth was a newlywed, technically at least. And in many ways, she was still enjoying herself. But right at the moment her mind was spinning, her heart still thumping because Neil Diamond had paid her an unspoken compliment. She had gladly received it and would have certainly welcomed more conversation from him on the subject, to the extent that she'd been reluctant to leave the studio. These feelings disturbed her. She was married. Shouldn't she be immune to such an exhilarating reaction?

"Oh, Leah, he's just . . . well, you know . . . he's just Carlton. No fireworks, no magic, but he's nice and he really is so talented."

"But, I mean, what do you love about him? What made you fall in love with him?"

Fall in love with him?

"Oh, who knows why people fall in love, Leah? Love is such an undefinable thing . . ." Elisabeth readjusted herself at the wheel, feeling suddenly restive.

They raced along Cahuenga toward Highland Avenue. The car veered toward Hollywood, where the three had agreed to cap off the evening with hot fudge sundaes at C. C. Brown's, home of the most outrageously decadent chocolate in Southern California.

"I have been in love so many times," Carmen's rich accent added emphasis to her observations as she laughed at her younger friends' dialogue. "And it's always something different. It's one

101

man's laugh. It's another man's eyes. It's his movements or his words . . ."

"Or his bank account, dear Carmen. Don't forget his bank account!" Leah smiled a little bitterly, warming to the subject. "Fact is, they're all alike. We want them to cherish us, admire us, pamper us, whatever. And what do they want? To get us into bed, of course. The rest is just formality!"

"I wouldn't say Carlton is really like that at all," Elisabeth frowned.

Carmen and Leah exchanged an almost imperceptible look. Elisabeth noticed it, but was unwilling to listen to any further discussion. Finding herself on unfamiliar footing, she abruptly changed the subject.

"C.C.'s makes the best fudge sauce on earth, and I, for one, am going to enjoy it. Don't you two ever think about anything but men?"

Elisabeth turned up the desk light and pulled her paper closer to it. It always seemed dark in Carlton's enchanted cottage, no matter how many lights she turned on. She examined a poem she had begun in September. Was it worth finishing?

> There is a time of fadings
> A strange, golden brittleness
> That men call autumn
> When all that has been begins to slip away,
> And longing fills the eyes with tears,
> As the soul grasps at something
> Already lost, long since out of reach . . .

The phone rang.

"Oh, hi, Carlton."

"Elisabeth, we're going to wrap up this meeting a little early, and I want you to do me a favor. Could you tidy things up a bit and make some of that wonderful chowder of yours? I'm bringing a friend home for dinner."

Elisabeth sighed but managed to sound delighted. She'd hoped to spend the evening writing. "Sure, Carlton, how long will you be?"

"Oh, I'd say you've got an hour and a half. Will that be okay?"

Dear Carlton, what you really mean to say is, "Don't embarrass me with a messy house and no soup."

"That's fine, of course. Who are you bringing? Anyone I know?"

"No, you don't know him yet. But you'll be extremely glad to meet him, Elisabeth."

Carlton's voice sounded unusually merry and inspired Elisabeth to make extra efforts in her preparations. She located a new box of creamy white candles and replaced the half-burned ones in all the brass candleholders. She dusted, swept, and lit fires in both fireplaces. She rushed out to the market for chowder supplies and, just before the two men arrived, put on a long calico dress with a white pinafore that made her feel like a medieval heroine.

Moments later, the front door opened. Accompanying Carlton was a tiny man with a dapper goatee and twinkling green eyes. "Elisabeth, I'd like you to meet James Novack. He's an antiques dealer and an artist, and as you recall, he owns Le Tour in Laguna. James, my wife Elisabeth."

James laughed with delight when he saw her. "You're perfect. You match the house. How marvelous!"

James Novack, like Stephen Andre, was evidently gay. His speech, his mannerisms, and his walk were reminiscent of others who had opted for an "alternative lifestyle." In the years since Glen Oaks, California and Los Angeles Bible College, Elisabeth had learned to recognize particular characteristics in various men, and to expect to find homosexuals in certain roles.

In the retail business, for example, display trimmers, fashion designers, cosmetic consultants, and hair stylists seemed committed to developing fresh nuances of effeminacy. Meanwhile, there were always rumors of transvestites modeling size eight designer gowns, who made profound and lasting impressions upon all who saw them backstage in their pantyhose.

The television industry featured choreographers, male dancers, wardrobe designers, and a large number of art directors and set decorators who had a predilection for homosexuality and made a concerted effort to communicate it. By now, on the west side of Los Angeles, the "closet" was passé, except among married bisexuals.

Since Elisabeth's marriage to Carlton, their social life seemed to be populated with more gay men than with heterosexuals, a phenomenon that made her feel out of place. Still, it seemed logical, considering the way of the world in Hollywood. So, all things considered, James Novack's particular presence was not unfamiliar to her and not at all disturbing.

As a matter of fact, the two took an immediate liking to each other. He walked over and kissed her on the cheek. "Carlton, you've found yourself a beauty!" He seemed genuinely delighted.

Carlton always looked pleased when another man paid attention to his wife. Smiling, he inquired about the status of dinner. "She makes fabulous chowder. You'll love it," he said as he dramatically presented her with a bright bouquet of red and white roses and baby's breath.

How come you only bring me flowers when someone important comes to dinner?

"Thanks, Carlton! How nice." She smiled as she handed them back to him, knowing that he would prefer to arrange them in a vase himself. Her floral creations never quite suited him. Thankfully, she fared better with her cooking.

In the past few months, Elisabeth had developed three or four foolproof, socially acceptable recipes for entertaining Carlton's friends and associates. The Baptist potluck casseroles Lucilla had taught her to prepare were unquestionably gauche in a world of pâtés, cassoulets, and paellas. Instead, she'd quickly learned that a fragrant soup, an unusual salad, a freshly baked loaf, and a bottle of good wine satisfied the cosmopolitan taste of just about anyone.

James followed her into the kitchen while Carlton took off his tie and then busied himself with the roses. "I understand you know about my Laguna house."

She smiled at him radiantly. "You can't imagine how amazing it is to meet you. You see, when I was a little girl . . ."

She hesitated wondering just how much he needed to know.

"Tell me the whole story!" James pulled up a chair, fixed his gaze on her face, and waited expectantly.

"Well, you see, I was quite ill as a child. And as a teenager, I wasn't expected to live. Just after a very serious bout of illness, my parents took me to Laguna Beach. We rented a little house right next to Victoria Cove.

"I was unbelievably unattractive and miserable then, and I lived in a kind of dream world. I saw your tower, James, and I told myself that someday . . ."

She paused, besieged by hot, unexpected tears.

He was still studying her as she spoke.

"Someday . . . of course, I was just a young kid . . . I thought I would marry the man who lived in the house and come sweeping down the tower in a beautiful gown!" She laughed nervously as she finished the story, hoping she hadn't said anything wrong.

James Novack, an incurable romantic, was swept away by the coincidence. "It's amazing! I absolutely love it! It's right out of a movie. Look, I want to give you something."

James stood up and reached his hand into his pocket. He pulled out a key ring and twisted off a silvery key. "Here. Take this. It's the key to Le Tour. I want you to have it. I'm back and forth to New York all the time. And when I'm gone, I want you to use the house—anytime you want to. I can't marry you . . ." he chuckled, glancing at Carlton who had just walked into the kitchen, "but I can make you the lady of the house, at least now and then."

Elisabeth stared at James, her hands shaking, her eyes flooded. "Are . . . are you sure?"

"Of course I'm sure! And I'm leaving for New York tomorrow. Why don't you go down for the weekend?"

"Carlton, would you mind?"

He shook his head, glad to see her so well occupied. "I'll be working anyway. Why don't you go ahead, Elisabeth."

After dinner, the room warmed with firelight and flickering candles, Elisabeth studied James Novack's face as he conversed with Carlton. He was really remarkably handsome and had a delightful personality.

What a waste. Oh well, at least this way I don't have to worry about marrying him!

The instant he and Carlton walked out the door and toward the street, she picked up the phone and dialed.

"Hello, Mr. Stephen? Hi. It's Elisabeth. Listen, I won't be able to work Saturday, I'm so sorry."

Carlton had placed his fragrant rose arrangement next to the phone. Unconsciously, she rubbed a red petal between her fingers as she spoke. What if Mr. Stephen said no? He wouldn't, would he?

"I have to go out of town unexpectedly. Oh, thank you for being so understanding."

"Oh, yes. I'll definitely be back on Monday. See you then. Thanks again . . ."

The drive to Laguna had seemed endless, thanks to Friday night traffic. Now, at last on the coast highway, Elisabeth clicked the right blinker on as she passed Rockledge and made a quick right turn downhill on Victoria Drive.

For once I won't have to worry about finding a parking place. Honestly, this is the strangest experience . . .

She slowed as she approached Le Tour. A black iron hanging sign marked the front gate. She timidly pulled into the carport, halfway expecting someone to come storming out, demanding that she leave.

No one appeared. She strengthened herself with the promise that she really wasn't imagining any of this, was she?

The sultry beach air was laden with sea scents and eucalyptus and warm with nostalgia. Not bothering with her bags, she slipped out of the driver's seat and, with the silvery key clutched tightly in her hand, all but tiptoed to the front door of the house. She slipped the key in the lock, her hand quivering. It turned. The door opened.

Hardly able to take a breath for fear of disturbing the miracle, Elisabeth walked into the most spectacular house she had ever seen. Lofty glass windows revealed a vast, blue-spangled view of the Pacific Ocean, while the interior boasted a collection of fine art unlike anything she'd ever laid eyes on outside a museum. There were antiques here, yes, but not the predictable English country relics that Carlton and his other friends demanded.

Here was a Victorian chair. There was an Edwardian armoire. A contemporary glass table gleamed in the dining room, and over it, in all its eclectic splendor, hung an absolutely enormous brass chandelier, bearing no less than a dozen red wax candles. A beamed cathedral ceiling soared two stories above her, and an immense stone fireplace faced her, large enough to grace a castle.

Once her heart stopped pounding, Elisabeth's ears were filled with two gentler sounds—the ticking of several vintage clocks and the endless roaring of the sea. And, wonder of wonders, above all else she could see the top of a European tower. The Victoria Beach tower. *Her* tower. It was waiting, there at the end of a flower-bordered path.

Not wasting a moment, and following James' instructions explicitly, she located the key and rushed toward the turret. Entering at the top, she carefully made her way down the spiral steps. At the bottom, she opened the door, and nearly collided with two small children huddled on the steps above the rising tide.

They stared at her in wonderment, the incarnation of a local children's myth. "Is it your tower? Can we go inside? Please? Just till the waves stop?"

Smiling at some past illusion of her own, Elisabeth gathered the little girls inside. There they waited until a thundering series of large breakers subsided.

"You'd better go now," she said to them, "while the water is quiet. Otherwise more big waves will come, and you'll be in trouble."

The children scampered away, thankful to the fairy-tale princess for keeping them dry and safe.

Elisabeth spun around for one last quick look, whispered farewell to her beach, and promised to be back in the morning. She re-locked the door, returned to the carport, and gathered up her clothes. Intending to spend the evening listening to music and writing, she built a small fire, lit a few candles, and tried to find an FM station on James' stereo. The signal cut in and out, but she left a popular music station on anyway, afraid to try to operate the turntable.

I've got to call Mother. She won't believe where I am.

She picked up the phone and dialed Oregon. Harold had retired, and he and Lucilla had left the California metropolis to join two of his brothers in the next state north.

"Mother! Guess where I am."

"I can't imagine. Where?"

"I'm staying in the house with the tower at Victoria Beach in Laguna. The owner is a friend of Carlton's, and he actually gave me the key. Can you believe that?"

"No, I can't! What kind of a man is he?"

"Oh, he's really nice. I like him a lot. He's a gay man who works in film . . ."

"Gay?"

"You know, homosexual. But he's really . . ."

"Elisabeth, you'll get a disease if you stay there!"

"A disease?"

"The towels! The sheets! How could you stay in a place like that?"

The conversation ended rather sourly just seconds later. *Mother probably never intended to spend her life throwing cold water on me. But she always does it. Always! Every single time I get excited about anything. Why do I bother to call?*

Shaking her head, Elisabeth walked toward the windows, where a breathtaking sunset was painting the sea and sky a thousand shades of golden pink.

My folks weren't so thrilled with my marriage to Carlton, but if I hadn't married him, I wouldn't have met James. And if I hadn't met James, I'd have never made it inside this house!

Dreams do come true! They just don't always come true quite the way you think they're going to.

She unpacked her bag, removing a colorful velour gown, the perfect costume for a perfect night. Just as she was pulling it over her head, "Hello, My Friend, Hello" crackled across the radio. She stopped, laughed out loud, and turned it off.

Neil Diamond! Leah, your imagination is even worse than mine! Anyway, some dreams make more sense than others.

Rummaging through her bag for a pair of slippers, she was surprised to find her old LABC Bible, never unpacked from some earlier journey.

It must be six months since I've even looked at this! Mother would be horrified.

Wistfully, she thumbed through the delicate, well-worn pages, remembering childhood times when she had pored over them, seeking help. Today no help was necessary. All was well. She was in "her" house at last, and the eternal sounds of the sea and the passing of time were her only companions.

A clock rang out, then seconds later, another. *Clever James. He has them set so they don't all chime at once. And what difference does it make anyway? Who cares what time it is in a place like this?*

She started to close the Bible, and just as she did, an under-lined proverb caught her eye.

"The name of the Lord is a strong tower; the righteous runneth into it, and is safe."

She didn't remember having marked it with red ink. She couldn't imagine what it might have meant to her a lifetime ago. But as she considered the words, she lifted her eyes to the window, toward the silhouette of the old stone tower, fading quickly into the deepening darkness. An unexpected sense of excitement stirred inside her. A faint longing rippled through her.

I wonder what it means, "The name of the Lord is a strong tower." That's a strange choice of words.

Shrugging, she set the Bible aside and stretched out across James' king size brass bed. Still another clock chimed. It was somewhere around eight, but the sea's song was a powerful tranquilizer. Elisabeth drifted off, and for the rest of the night her mind was flooded with mighty waves, higher than Victoria Beach's massive cliffs.

In her dreams she was a child once more, scurrying through rising tides. More and more afraid, little Betty Fuller was desperately seeking a place of refuge from increasingly dangerous tides. Climbing across deeply shadowed crags and crevasses, she could find no place to hide from the gathering, destructive breakers.

7

Are you sure I look all right?" Elisabeth smoothed the leg of her crepe jumpsuit for the hundredth time, hoping to eradicate any wrinkles that might mar its ebony splendor. She was a vision in black and silver, rhinestones twinkling in her ears, her lips and nails glossy red.

"Stop worrying, Elisabeth! You're just fine. You really couldn't look better, dear."

Now what is that supposed to mean? And don't call me "dear," either.

Irritability carved a furrow between her eyes, and only with concentrated effort was she able to smooth it away. Just then the world spun, then came to an uncertain stop. Elisabeth's hands grew clammy, and terror raced through her body. For weeks such attacks of vertigo had been occurring, sometimes accompanied by severe shortness of breath. What was wrong with her?

Carlton was never one to lavish compliments on his wife, and seemed to carefully avoid the words "beautiful" or "fabulous" when considering her appearance. Fortunately, Elisabeth heard those words often enough at work to alleviate most of her uncertainties. But tonight was different. They were about to arrive at a holiday fete where no amount of finery in the world could possibly create in her a sense of belonging.

Bob Hope's San Fernando Valley home spread itself in vast, unpretentious comfort across a wooded lot, adjacent to his beloved Toluca Lake Country Club golf course. That year, the famous comedian was hosting a Christmas party in California instead of visiting far-flung military bases with his usual traveling road show. The Caseys arrived at a house that was ablaze with lights and sparkling with celebrities.

Dolores Hope greeted Elisabeth and Carlton and took several minutes to show them around her home. She was especially fond of crèches, which she had collected from all around the world. The various handmade nativity scenes brought a sacred touch to an otherwise secular event.

Mrs. Hope was a stately lady who had weathered many a Hollywood storm and apparently emerged unscathed. Her gracious manner and warm hospitality belied the fact that she didn't know Elisabeth Casey from any other stranger on earth, and she most assuredly wouldn't remember her tomorrow.

The evening had been planned for months, and because of his position in "the business," Carlton had appeared on the guest list rather early on. Although he didn't work on the Hope shows himself, he was part of a circle of directors and producers who were thought to be socially significant.

After receiving a friendly welcome, the scores of guests began to circulate, drinks in hand, sharing tales of television intrigue and memories of the "old days." Venerable USO show veterans were surrounded by admirers, while up-and-coming starlets, actors, and writers edged their way toward their successful counterparts, hoping for a boon or a blessing.

An endless array of lavish food tables exhibited fruits, cheeses, and international gourmet delicacies. And to the delight of all the guests who "knew," Chasen's of Beverly Hills had supplied everyone's favorite chile—surely enough to feed several hungry Mexican villages.

Despite the hours she'd spent in cosmetic preparation, Elisabeth approached the evening almost paralyzed by her own private insecurities. A fixed smile ached around her mouth, and words froze in her throat. Her clothes felt as if they were wearing her. Her hand shook as she clutched her obligatory glass of Chablis.

Elisabeth's year-old marriage to Carlton had taken a strange toll on her self-confidence, a quality that had been meager enough to begin with. Now, besides daily struggles with her past difficulties, a constant sense of inadequacy haunted her. Carlton never appeared to be quite satisfied with her—her looks, her words, her efforts. It was undefinable and really undiscussable. Was it her twisted perception or his warped perspective? Either way, an erosion was taking place, a steady stream of fear eating away at the person of Elisabeth.

She sat alone, watching the crowd. She knew only a handful of people there, and they were not really friends but business acquaintances with whom Carlton was already engrossed in conversation. It was a fascinating scene to observe, this beautifully produced festivity. And yet another unique performance was about to unfold—a special concert by the Marine Corps band, of all things. When Bob Hope threw a party, he threw a party!

Under a white canopy in the back garden, the red-and-blue uniformed instrumentalists were gathering, and soon the crowd began to move toward them. Elisabeth arose and walked toward the music. The Marine Corps Hymn filled the chilly night air. "From the halls of Montezuma . . ."

Too bad Daddy couldn't be here. They're playing his song.

Her eyes moved from face to face. What did these young military men think about Hollywood? Were they attracted or amused? Did they see this as an evening to remember or some sort of inside joke? She looked from the trumpet section to the woodwinds, from the drums to the . . .

What? Playing a drum? It can't be! But isn't that . . . Jerry Baldwin!

Did her eyes deceive her? Standing behind a snare drum was a familiar face, very familiar indeed. How many times had she stared at it from the piano bench? It was him all right. No question about it.

How could she catch his eye? There. He was looking at her! His eyes studied her momentarily, then moved away without a glimmer of recognition. Maybe it wasn't him after all. But it was. It was!

Surely I don't look that different. But then, I guess I do. I haven't seen him since my skin got well. That's got to be it. He just doesn't know me anymore!

After several Christmas carols, the band took an intermission. Forgetting her earlier fears, Elisabeth excused herself repeatedly as she wended her way through the crowd toward the Marines.

"Jerry!" Her voice croaked in her ears. She cleared her throat and tried again. "Jerry!"

He turned and looked at her blankly. "Aren't you Jerry Baldwin?"

"Yeah, I'm Jerry." His Marine companions were smiling by now, thoroughly enjoying the sight of a beautiful woman pursuing one of their own.

"You don't recognize me, do you? I'm Elisa . . . I'm Betty. Betty Fuller? From church?"

"Betty? From church? No way!" Jerry was at a loss for words. "What happened to you?"

Elisabeth felt like an impostor wearing a disguise. "Well, my skin was healed . . ." She started to explain, but after briefly considering it, she wondered if her theology of the miraculous would elude him.

"I can't believe my eyes. You're the most beautiful woman in the room. I didn't know you had it in you, Betty! . . ."

"Well, last time I saw you, you weren't exactly wearing a Marine Corps uniform yourself. Or playing a snare drum, I might add. Tell me about yourself."

Jerry had always been attractive, but now his good looks were enhanced by a suave, well-rehearsed style—the touch of a warm hand, the wink of an eye. His brief biographical monologue was frequently punctuated with, "You are so pretty, I can't believe it," and "I can't take my eyes off you."

Like a parched plant, Elisabeth absorbed his words and gestures thirstily. Her very being began to glow with renewed life.

They talked for fifteen minutes, until the band played again. Then they talked some more. Wanting to be honest, she told him she was married, but she wasn't quite sure if he heard. Before long it was time for the Marines to reboard their bus and head back to their lodging. "Betty, how can I get hold of you? We've got so much more to talk about." He spoke the words softly, almost conspiratorially.

She enthusiastically wrote her phone number on a tiny piece of paper. "Come see me at work if you can. I model at Bullock's Wilshire. Here's the address—1050 Wilshire Boulevard."

"I'll try. But I might not get back into L.A. for awhile. Anyway, I'll call you." He scribbled a phone number and his mailing address on another scrap of paper. "Listen, let's keep in touch. Seeing you is the best thing that's happened to me in months!"

"Of course we'll keep in touch, Jerry." She chuckled wryly. "After all, there's no friend like an old friend . . ."

He gently placed his hand to the side of her face. He brushed back her hair and kissed her, ever so softly, on the cheek. He looked at her, gravely, for just a moment, then turned and walked away into the December night.

The models' room mirror reflected a regal Elisabeth Casey, garbed in a pearl-strewn satin bridal gown, veiled in pure silk lace. With Leah's help, she swept out the door and onto the runway, to the appreciative applause of the Tea Room crowd.

I wish Jerry could see me now. Maybe he's here today!

Although she knew better, she couldn't resist scanning the room. Ever since the Bob Hope party, Jerry Baldwin had so obsessed her thoughts that she could barely concentrate on anything else. She'd misplaced her car keys half a dozen times, nearly wrecked the white Jaguar, and lost six or seven pounds within a week's time.

The Monday following the party, Jerry had boldly sent an enormous arrangement of flowers to her in the models' room. Much to the delight of the other girls the accompanying note read, "Until we meet again. Love, Jerry." At last Elisabeth was up to something, too! She, herself, was only slightly chagrined, more swept away with pleasure than worried about the extramarital implications of the bouquet.

"He's just an old friend," she feebly responded to their oohs and aahs. "No big deal."

"You can't fool me, Elisabeth. You've been walking on clouds ever since you saw him. I say you're in love, no matter what you want to call it!" Carmen, the consummate expert on such matters, concluded her assessment by reapplying her lip gloss and brushing her shiny, black hair.

Now, as Elisabeth reentered the models' room in the bridal gown, she looked at the flowers thoughtfully.

What a strange world. I'm dressed like a bride, but there's no wedding. I'm married, but I really don't have a husband. I'm getting flowers from a man, but there's no hope for the future.

A wave of vertigo swayed her. Tiny, bright lights exploded across her vision. Her hands began to sweat as she took off the gown, and sat down at her place, her chin resting in her hands. The soaring ecstasy she'd experienced after Jerry's reappearance began its slow, heavy descent.

He'd sent the flowers, yes, but why hadn't he called her? Had he forgotten about her? What did it all mean? Was she on his mind as much as he was on hers? And what difference did it all make, anyway?

"What's wrong Elisabeth?" Leah's sweet face looked worried. "You're really pale, kiddo. What's wrong?"

"I don't know what's wrong with me. I've been having these dizzy spells. Maybe I'm not eating right or something. Do you ever feel kind of short of breath and dizzy? I've been seeing these funny shooting stars, too . . ."

Leah shook her head and sat down next to her friend. "Sounds like nerves to me. Are you worried about this Jerry thing?"

"No, not really. It's just fun to dream. You know what I mean?"

"You'd better be careful, Elisabeth. When *you* dream, your dreams have a way of coming true!"

Another wave of dizziness. Elisabeth laid her head down for a moment.

"Maybe you should see a doctor. You're not pregnant, are you?"

"No . . . no way. We haven't done anything since my last period. No, I think maybe you're right, I'm just tense or something. I told you my mother has cancer, didn't I?"

Leah nodded. Elisabeth had told her about her mother's illness three times now, obviously shattered by the news. It was odd, considering the fact that Lucilla and her daughter had nothing whatsoever in common. Then Elisabeth had a sudden thought, and turned to Carmen. "Got any Valium?"

Carmen laughed as she opened her cluttered drawer and pulled out a bejeweled pillbox. "But of course! Voilà!" She opened it to reveal several small, white tablets. "Good idea, Elisabeth. Take one. Take two! I've got a million more at home."

Elisabeth filled a paper cup at the water cooler. Her hands shaking, she swallowed the little pill. For the rest of the afternoon, she felt noticeably better.

Just before the models headed home, she walked over to Carmen's place. "By the way, Carmen, before you go, would you mind giving me a couple more of those Valium? That one really helped."

Carmen poured the remaining five pills into her friend's palm. "I'll bring you a couple dozen more tomorrow. I get them free from a doctor friend of ours. They won't hurt you. They're only ten milligrams each."

Leah responded to a knock on the door, finding the Tea Room hostess outside. "Somebody's here to see Elisabeth," she announced. "A soldier or something . . ."

Leah beamed at Elisabeth triumphantly. "Good thing you took that Valium. You're going to need it!"

Elisabeth walked out the door, speechless. She rounded the corner, and there, in uniform, stood Jerry.

He caught his breath when she appeared. "I swear, you're beautiful!"

She shook her head as he took her in his arms. "You don't believe me, do you?"

"Oh, I think you believe it . . ."

It was a long embrace, longer than they intended.

"Betty, where can we talk? I was going to call, but there was so much to say . . . I drove all the way here from Pendleton. I have to talk to you!"

She led him to a table into the empty restaurant. "You want some coffee?"

He nodded. Once the waitress left, he sat staring at Elisabeth for several seconds before he blurted out the question. "Do you feel the way I do?"

"What do you mean, Jerry?"

"I mean I've thought of nothing but you since the Hope party. I wake up thinking about you. I go to sleep thinking about you. If you don't feel the same, I don't know what I'll do!"

Never in her life had Elisabeth heard such words. She stared at the handsome Marine, transfixed.

Why play games?

"Jerry, I don't know what to say. You know I'm married, but yes, I've been pretty preoccupied myself. I don't know what to think about all this. It's so strange, considering that we knew each other before and yet it was never like this . . ."

"*You* were never like this!"

Elisabeth studied his face for a moment. A flash of frustration stung her eyes, but she quieted herself. It was true, of course. Lucilla had always told her that no one would want her the way she was before. No one had, and certainly not Jerry.

"Well, the future doesn't hold much promise, Jerry. I'm married and you're in the service. What kind of relationship can we have?"

"All I want to do is hold you in my arms. Just seeing you, it seems like my life finally makes sense. The past, the present . . . oh, I don't know. I just want to hold you." His voice broke. "I've never felt this way before."

She reached across the table and took his hand in hers. "Jerry, we'll just have to be creative, I guess. I don't want to get into trouble with you. But I don't want to let go, either."

"Do you love me? Betty, tell me you love me."

"I . . . I hardly know you, but I've sure had you on my mind, Jerry." She took a breath.

Oh, why not just say it?

"Of course I love you."

Their conversation continued in much the same vein for several more minutes. Then Jerry looked at his watch. "Look, I can't stay here much longer or I'll get stuck in traffic. Walk down to my car with me, okay?"

In the far corner of the parking lot they said good-bye. Almost savagely, Jerry kissed Elisabeth's face, her lips, her hair, and held her against his chest until her neck hurt. "Until next time, I love you," he murmured as he left.

At twilight, sitting at the oak desk in Carlton's enchanted cottage, in a stiff, agonized hand Elisabeth wrote a simple poem.

> There is no mighty thunder with this deluge
> No angry rumbling heaven shakes my world and cries out
> Why?
> When and Why?
> Instead with bitter rhythm
> But gentle as constant freezing rain on brittle leaves
> Is Time's toneless heartless whisper:
> This is that which could have been
> This is that which would have been
> This is that which should have been.

Half-blinded by tears of despair, she could hardly read the lines back to herself. Even now, hours after he'd left her, she could still taste Jerry's cologne on her trembling lips.

The Laguna house throbbed with noise and laughter. James Novack was commemorating his fiftieth birthday, and everyone he could think of had been invited. When Carlton and Elisabeth arrived, the party was well underway. More than a dozen celebrants had spent the night there, getting an early start. Two gay couples necked on the living room couch. A circle of young men passed a joint around on the outside deck. Bar glasses tinkled, and smoke hung heavily in the humid air.

Elisabeth had taken two of Carmen's Valium before leaving Hollywood at about noon. She was determined never again to experience the inhibited, fearful feelings that had so disabled her at the Hope party. Now, entering the room in a somewhat dazed state of mind, she was aware of the "stars" that shot across her eyes now and then, but paid them little mind.

Despite the electrifying changes that Jerry had brought into her world, Elisabeth's physical discomforts had far from vanished. Lately some sort of lingering stomach upset had compounded her other symptoms, causing her to lose four more pounds. Friends were starting to accuse her of being marginally anorexic.

"You're turning into quite the hypochondriac, Elisabeth," Carlton had muttered on the way to Laguna. "Just because your mother's ill doesn't mean you have to fall apart, too."

Oh, dear Carlton, you are such an understanding man, aren't you? Well, what you don't know won't hurt you.

The more Elisabeth concentrated on Jerry and his passionate desire for her, the more disgusted she grew with Carlton. His undemonstrative personality was a constant source of irritation, and his personal disinterest in her was underscored by Jerry's constant inquiries and compliments. Even the way Carlton looked at his watch annoyed her! Little wonder that she and

Jerry were in touch by phone every day, whispering loving words across the miles between Hollywood Hills and Camp Pendleton.

James' party was the last social event the Caseys would attend before leaving for Europe the following week—Elisabeth's first trip abroad. Although in past reveries she often wandered through the fabled British Isles, she was presently more interested in keeping in touch with Jerry than in crossing the Atlantic. No matter. They would soon be on their way.

Just as she and Carlton entered the house, James caught Elisabeth's eye and beckoned her to come across the room. "This is my sister Bernice, Elisabeth. She's from Northern California, and I think you're just the person for her to know!"

Bernice was a shy, unassuming brunette of about thirty-five, whose only resemblance to her brother was in the blue of her eyes. "I'm so glad to meet you, Elisabeth. Jimmy told me all about you."

"Jimmy?"

James flushed slightly. "Oh, you know how families are. I'll bet you're "Betty" to your parents, right?"

Right. To my parents and Jerry.

"You're right, I'm Betty, all right. Has Bernice seen the beach yet?"

"Not yet! Why don't you take her down there?"

Glad for an excuse to leave the chaotic din behind, the two women made their way down the old tower and out onto the sand.

"Where are you from, Bernice?"

"Oh, my husband and I live in Palo Alto. We've got a couple of kids at Stanford. In fact, to tell you the truth, I've really got them on my mind. I probably shouldn't have left my daughter to come down here."

"Is she sick?"

"Yeah, I guess you could say that. She's a little . . . well, suicidal. She tried to kill herself two weeks ago."

"Oh, Bernice! How terrible!"

"Well, it's nothing new, really." Bernice sighed sadly. "She's been experimenting with drugs for three years, and that's what triggered the episode."

"Is anyone getting through to her?"

"Our pastor has been really helpful. He's young and has been through the drug scene himself. He's trying to steer her toward the Lord and away from her self-destructive attitude."

Elisabeth noticed a tiny gold cross at Bernice's throat. "Do you . . . are you . . . ?" She mutely pointed at the cross.

Bernice understood immediately. "Oh, yes. We're a very strong Christian family. That's what makes Shelley's situation so tough."

"What about . . ." She glanced up toward the house to make sure they were alone. "James?"

"Oh, Jimmy. Yes, well, as I'm sure you've noticed, he's a far cry from being a Christian. Our parents are heartbroken over him. He grew up in the church, of course, but he got involved with an older homosexual when he was a freshman in high school. And that was it—no turning back. But we're still praying for him. I really love Jimmy."

"Oh, so do I! I think he's wonderful! He's a terrific, lovable person." In no way did Elisabeth want to sound religious, yet she felt she should give Bernice her full support. "I'll pray for him, too," she said softly.

"Oh, thank you so much!" Bernice seemed exceptionally excited. "You know, I never expected to find another Christian at Jimmy's birthday party! What a surprise! Normally, I hate being around his friends. Imagine that—a Christian!"

To her horror, Elisabeth recoiled. Part of it might simply have been due to Bernice's overenthusiasm. But there was something else as well.

Why am I uncomfortable being identified as a Christian? I've called myself a Christian all my life! Elisabeth instantly assessed her thoughts. Was she ashamed of the faith and beliefs the word implied? Not really. No, that wasn't it at all.

It's them! It's Mother and Daddy and Rev. Turner and all the rest of them. They're Christians, and I want nothing to do with them.

In retrospect, the whole Bethany Baptist congregation seemed more dead than alive. Elisabeth desperately wanted to be alive.

"Well . . ." she hoped she hadn't taken too long to respond, "I'm pretty surprised to meet you here, too. My husband is . . . he goes to church sometimes, but that's about it."

"What's his name?"

"Carlton Casey. He's a television director."

"Oh, I've heard of him for years. He's a real close friend of Jimmy's, isn't he? You know, for some reason I thought . . . I must have misunderstood . . ."

A thundering wave crashed against the rocks, interrupting Bernice mid-sentence. The tide was swiftly rising, and the two headed back up the stairs, locking the beach door behind them. By now the party was wilder than ever. Two men were dancing cheek to cheek, fondling each other every few seconds, all to the hysterical laughter of their friends.

Elisabeth eased herself into a big chair, vaguely detached from the lusty scene unfolding around her. All of a sudden a thoroughly inebriated man plopped down next to her, perched on the edge of the same chair. She looked at him in dismay, but he merely hung his head, lost in melodrama.

"Don was my lover for twenty years," he mourned, tears pouring down his face. "Now look at him. He's just going from one boy to the next. He's breaking my heart."

She stared at him blankly, then at the dancing couple—Don and his latest flame. A strange, disconcerted feeling stirred in the pit of her stomach. What words of comfort could possibly be said under these bizarre circumstances? She glanced around the room. Carlton, as usual, was involved in an intense conversation. Bernice was nowhere to be seen.

Just then James sauntered by, drunk but happy. He glanced

at Don and his partner, then winked at Elisabeth. "We're a sick bunch, aren't we?" With that he laughed loudly, with the utmost glee.

Jerry. Jerry's normal. Where is he? Maybe I can reach him by phone.

She abruptly excused herself and rushed into James' bedroom, just in time to interrupt a passionate embrace between two long-haired college boys. "Oh, I'm sorry." They rolled their eyes and left, hand in hand.

She dialed a Camp Pendleton number she knew by heart. No answer. Where was Jerry? Was he trying to reach her? Longing for him overwhelmed her. She wanted to cry, to run, to hide in his arms and be safe. She hadn't seen him since their torrid farewell in the Bullock's Wilshire parking lot. Would it be the same if they met again?

Maybe I dialed wrong. God, please . . .

She tried again. Still no answer. Disappointment surged through her.

Why would God help me anyway? He's got to be disgusted with me. I wonder which is worse, being at this party or being in love with a man who isn't my husband.

She sat alone in the darkened bedroom, lost in thought for more than ten minutes. When she found her way back into the living room, a stand-up comic had taken "center stage" and was doing one of his routines.

"Did you hear the one about the evangelist and Miss Texas? The evangelist says, 'I'm gonna save this girl! I'm gonna save this girl!'

"The deacon says, 'You gonna save this girl, preacher?'

"'That's right, brother! I'm gonna save this girl till after church, when I've got plenty of time to enjoy her!'"

The response to the lame joke was predictably uproarious.

A series of "evangelist" stories continued, each one raunchier than the one before, all depicting Elmer-Gantry-style caricatures. Elisabeth sat in silence, unamused and saddened.

Reminiscence transported her across nearly three decades, past LABC, beyond Glen Oaks High School, all the way back to a hot summer California night during the sixth year of her life. She saw herself, a blonde tot dressed in ruffles, sitting between her parents in a revival tent.

A Southern Baptist evangelist had stood sweating in the pulpit, holding a Bible in the open palm of his hand, and pointing at the congregation with the other. He had been loud and fiery, and his words rang with warning. But he'd had a kindly face and eyes that shone with sincerity.

Elisabeth could still hear him saying, "If you'll repent from your sins and invite the Lord Jesus into your heart, you'll have everlasting life. If you don't, you're headed for eternal punishment. It's up to you, brothers and sisters. Won't you come now and give your lives to the Lord?"

She tugged on Harold's arm and whispered, "Daddy, can I go?"

"Go where?"

"I want to invite Jesus into my heart."

The people in the tent began singing "Just As I Am." Harold looked at Lucilla, who shrugged and nodded. They each took their daughter by the hand and led her up the sawdust aisle to the altar. The evangelist met them there.

"Why are y'all here?" he asked Harold.

"My daughter wanted to come up."

The man knelt down and gently took her hand in his. "What's your name, Sugar? Why is it you came forward?"

"I'm Betty, and I want Jesus to live in my heart."

"Do you understand what that means?"

She'd nodded.

"Say your verse for him, Betty," Lucilla prodded, smiling proudly.

"For God so loved the world that He . . . that He . . ." Shaky and scared, she'd forgotten the rest of the words.

"He gave His only begotten Son . . ." Lucilla prompted.

Now Betty had remembered. ". . . gave His only begotten Son that whosoever believeth on Him should not perish but have everlasting life."

"That's right. Do you believe in Jesus?"

"Yes."

"Well then, invite Him into your heart."

"Do I just ask Him?"

"That's all you have to do."

She'd closed her eyes tightly. "Jesus, please come into my heart. Amen."

Afterward, little Betty had been wide-eyed with excitement, joyfully bound for heaven. Full of childlike faith, she'd ridden home that night watching the stars from the backseat of Harold's '58 Ford, firmly believing that Jesus would be her friend forever.

Now ribald laughter broke harshly into her thoughts, inspired by more crude humor. Unwilling to listen to another word, Elisabeth walked out onto the deck, trying to focus her attention on the sunset-stained ocean.

Carlton found her there, several minutes later. She looked at him, surprised that he had joined her. His mission was evidently not one of companionship. His face was uncharacteristically angry.

"Elisabeth, did you tell Bernice that you were going to pray for James' soul? Did you actually say that to her?"

"I . . . I . . . Carlton, she's a Christian, and we were talking about praying for her daughter. James' name came up. I never specifically said, 'I'm praying for James' soul.' No, I didn't. Why?"

"Elisabeth!" Carlton's voice was hard, edged with ice. "Everyone who knows James knows his sister is emotionally unstable. She's already told me you're praying for her brother. Next she'll tell him, and he'll never speak to either one of us again."

"Carlton, I don't think she's . . ."

"Shut up!" The expression on Carlton's face was unlike any she'd seen before. It reflected nothing short of hatred.

"You and your religion! Healings and voices and all the rest of your ravings! Why can't you go to church like the rest of us and then keep your big mouth shut!"

She was immobilized, shocked. *Why did I ever tell him any-thing? I should have known he wouldn't understand.* "Carlton, I thought you . . ."

"Shut up! Get your things. We're going home before you make an even bigger fool of yourself."

Disoriented, Elisabeth grabbed her handbag, said a quick good-bye to James, who barely noticed her, and rushed into the bathroom. She fought off a wave of nausea and managed to swallow two Valiums. Bending over the faucet, she washed them down with a flood of water.

Outside, Carlton grabbed her elbow and steered her through the door. Reeling with sorrow, Elisabeth took a last look at the wonderful house with the tower. In the background, in spite of the party noise, she could hear a clock chiming and ocean break-ers answering with their faraway, muted voices.

Would she ever again return?

8

How brightly, how brightly the stars shine tonight
On the skirts of the sky I am taking my flight
And I streak through the black like an insect in fright
I am going away, I am going away.

There are houses below with their families abed,
And they never will know that I passed overhead,
And they couldn't have heard when I quietly said,
"I am going away, I am going away."

I am going away on a storybook ride
From the quicksilver sea and the mercury tide
And I couldn't have stayed, and I shouldn't have tried.
I am leaving today, I am going away.

Elisabeth was safely buckled into the big Pan American jetliner, tears streaming down her face. She finished her poem with a great sense of satisfaction that, once again, her frustration and turmoil were recorded—just in case she ever wanted to recapture the agony. Even now, her present heartache was staring back at her from a sheet of notebook paper. It seemed to ease the hurt a little.

She glanced at Carlton, already sound asleep. More tears brimmed in her eyes. She was leaving Jerry behind at the rate of nearly five hundred miles per hour.

I promised him I'd try to write every day. I might as well start now.

The poem, she thought, she would keep to herself. Chewing on the end of her pen, she contemplated Jerry's potential appreciation of her writing. She'd never shown him a single poem, and deep inside she suspected he wouldn't care a great deal for poetry—after all, he was a Marine. Although her ex-Marine father had always treasured her verses, Elisabeth sensed that his interest was exceptional. Besides, letters would do just fine. She reached for a packet of blue air-letters in her carry-on bag and wrote,

Monday

Well, hello, my friend,

I always start things out with such good intentions. And here I am writing my first letter to you, from the plane, on my way to London.

LAX was crowded with its usual motley assortment of types. There was a five-hundred-pound man in a loud, plaid shirt; hundreds of polyester, drip-dry pant suits; even a lady I knew was there—she works at the Bi-Rite drug store in Westwood. She's English, you see, and going to London for four weeks.

Beyond that, there's not much to report, dear love. Two ladies just had a shouting match across the aisle from me, fighting fiercely about the air vents. In the meantime, I'm sitting here missing you.

That's about all I have to say now, but I'll write more tomorrow.

Love,
Betty

Elisabeth didn't bother recounting to Jerry that occasional strolls around the airplane seemed to counteract her restlessness. Every hour or so, she meandered through the plane, curiously observing the various passengers who were snoozing, reading, and chatting their way across the North Atlantic.

On one such excursion, she noticed that a row of bulkhead seats held a frantic young mother and her three children, all less than four years of age. The poor woman was trying to quiet her eldest, who persisted in shrieking at the most inopportune moments. Unfortunately, by the time Elisabeth arrived on the scene, the second child had joined the wailing. Meanwhile, the newborn infant in the mother's arms was fussing, constricting her movements, and making it impossible for her to resolve the rapidly escalating crisis.

"Can I help?" Elisabeth smiled at the woman and reached for the baby.

"Thank God you asked!"

Thank God I don't have kids! I just hope this one doesn't throw up all over me. Elisabeth glanced protectively at her new denim dress.

Then, in spite of herself, she smiled at the petite bundle. The fair-haired infant, clad in a kelly green sleepsuit, proudly displayed a minuscule Izod alligator on its chest.

"Is it a boy or a girl?"

"She's a girl. Her name is Brooke. She's six weeks old."

Good Lord. This could be the world's smallest yuppie.

"She's beautiful." Elisabeth touched her face softly.

"Yeah, but she's got that rash . . ."

"Rash? Where?"

"On her face. Don't you see it?"

Elisabeth squinted, and eventually discerned four or five nearly invisible bumps.

"That's a rash? I wouldn't worry about it if I were you."

Elisabeth sat down in an empty seat and cradled the baby in her arms while the weary mother dragged her other two indignant offspring down the aisle for a walk. Observing the infant's tiny pink face, Elisabeth was struck with the miracle of new life— a human being, so perfectly miniaturized.

Little as she is, you can already see that she looks like her brother and sister. I wonder who I looked like. I wonder if my mother studied my face and marveled at my existence. I wonder if Daddy smiled when he held me.

Elisabeth turned the child around onto her knees. Brooke opened two blue eyes and looked directly at the stranger who held her. A determined look crossed her face and she began to busy herself by jerking her hands around, kicking her legs, and making outlandish faces.

What am I going to do if she screams?

She didn't. At least not until her mother returned. "Thanks so much, I really appreciate your doing that. It's a long trip for these kids."

"Listen, ten hours in a plane is a long time for anyone to sit still. I don't envy you a bit."

In an odd way, however, Elisabeth did feel a pang of some sort. Maybe it wasn't envy, but it was a kind of faint regret.

Carlton and I will never have kids. No way. He'd never be able to tolerate them. I wonder if Jerry wants children . . .

With that, she was back in her seat, dreaming about Jerry again. Before long, the otherwise uneventful flight from L.A. was over, and Elisabeth's adventure in the British Isles was verifiably underway. She and Carlton checked into a fine hotel on the outskirts of London, an old manor with lovely gardens and woods nearby. They were to stay there for a few days, look around London, and then head for the English countryside, South Wales, and finally Ireland.

In the days to come, she documented her every experience in a series of heartfelt letters to Jerry. She dulled her anxieties and physical symptoms with Valium. And she experienced her first exposure to the kind of faraway places that had first come to her attention through her wonderful *Book of Marvels*. Even her dreary experience with English literature at LABC had put names like Canterbury and Stratford-upon-Avon and Laugharne on her lips.

So it was that, in spite of her melancholy romantic disposition, she was reluctantly excited. And, as promised, Elisabeth's first day was recorded on thin blue paper:

Tuesday

Hello, my dear Jerry!

London! I'm really in London! This magical, marvelous old town is a montage of cabs and red flags and bustling people—fruit stands, pubs, and Wimpy bars. My heart stops every time I pass through Trafalgar Square—I've always had a dream that someday something wonderful would happen to me there. I wish you'd suddenly appear among the pigeons!

Had lunch at the Cockney Pride pub in Picadilly. Rode the tube to London Tower. Explored old and new Bond Streets and the Burlington Arcade. At last Carlton bought me my long-sought-after blue sapphire ring! Not quite like the crown jewels, but it's fine for me. Tonight we see the London production of Noel Coward's *Design for Living,* starring Vanessa Redgrave.

Sorry, but now I must go down to the restaurant and meet Carlton. I'd really much prefer writing more to you but . . .

Much Love,
Betty

When Elisabeth arrived in the hotel dining room, Carlton was visiting with two graying Briton friends who seemed, if possible, even stuffier than he was. They barely acknowledged Elisabeth's arrival and continued their heady discussion about American movies.

"David Lean is a genius. *Dr. Zhivago* was truly a classic," one of them postulated. "It was a turning point. A landmark project, indeed."

Elisabeth had always loved the film version of Pasternak's novel, if sheerly from a romantic point of view. She took a second look at the man who spoke. He was as nondescript as a man in a frumpy suit and a toupee could be.

If he loves Dr. Zhivago, he can't be all bad.

"Oh, yes," the other man responded. He was equally bland in appearance, a condition that was relieved only by an utterly

137

tasteless chartreuse necktie. "The cinematography was really rather exceptional. Extraordinary camera work, wasn't it? I was most impressed by the remarkable commitment to detail!"

"Oh, yes. The detail. Did you notice the extravagant moldings in the apartment scene? Really marvelous, when you think about it. Most spectacular. I shall never forget those moldings!"

Cameras and moldings? What about the story? And the music? Who are these people, anyway?

As soon as it was even remotely possible, Elisabeth excused herself from this tiresome group and escaped to her room. Once there, she flipped on the television. Uninteresting films and an unfunny comedy show were her only options. She turned the set off. She'd already written to Jerry and wished fervently for something to read. To her surprise, there was a fairly current *National Geographic* in a bookcase. She was just settled down, ready to delve into it, when Carlton came back into the room.

"Did they leave already?"

"Yes, they're gone. We'd better get to sleep, Elisabeth. Tomorrow I want to be at Westminster Abbey first thing in the morning."

Elisabeth stuffed the *National Geographic* into her bag and obediently got ready for bed. By sundown the next day, she had written a full report to Jerry.

Wednesday

Hello, dear one.

Westminster Abbey is very crowded, but one can isolate oneself. I was somehow touched by the reading of the Lord's Prayer during the requested morning silence. Light streamed in through those remarkable windows and cast lovely patterns on the floor.

And Poet's Corner? Writer after writer is buried there, each one honored for his contributions to literature. How wonderful to be there, right next to them all! Surely *they* would have understood our needs and dreams and yearnings! Sad to say, many of them destroyed their lives trying to fulfill those very things.

Now I am on the boat going down the Thames from London to Kew Gardens. After a half hour in the wind, I have gone below deck to the dining area. Why is there such a sense of fascination in the steaming of tea cups, chilly air, and the motion of a moving boat?

During a quick lunch at the Markham, we met a Chelsea pensioner. He was a colorful old gentleman, a Dickensonian character with his broken-blood-vesseled cheeks, bright blue eyes, and proud uniform. He said he knew we were foreigners—it was stamped all over us.

Don't you sometimes wonder how others see us?

> All my love,
> Betty

Forty-eight hours later, the Chelsea pensioner long forgotten, Elisabeth and Carlton were slowly making their way through South Wales, across the Irish Sea, and onto the fabled Emerald Isle. The beautiful landscapes left Elisabeth nearly breathless. As a matter of fact, despite her faithful use of Valium, a sort of asthmatic wheeze and a disconcerting dizziness were, by now, actually taking her breath away. During the day, the condition was nothing more than uncomfortable. But at night, fear accompanied the symptoms, and she felt almost as if she might be suffocating.

"Carlton . . ." Sometimes she'd whisper his name when terror clutched at her heart. But she never found the courage to wake him up.

He'll think I'm crazy if I tell him I can't breathe. Besides, it'll go away. It always does.

Elisabeth's daily communication with Carlton wasn't so much strained as it was unremittingly insipid. The man seemed to be conversant about nothing but antique shops, clothing, historical buildings, and whatever points of interest were featured in the RAC *Guide to the British Isles.* The couple's dialogues were, therefore, reduced to rehashed reports of sights, sounds, and foods.

She asked herself the same question nearly everyday. *Why is he such a bad communicator? He's got to be the most boring man on earth. But maybe he can't help it. Maybe he just doesn't have anything to say.*

Naturally this mental course led her musings across the sea, back to the familiar dreams that starred Jerry. She focused her concentration on him day in and day out. During one particular Irish downpour, she even found herself getting up in the middle of the night and writing a poem. How she longed to send it to him! Would he understand?

She read and reread it to herself, trying to imagine his reaction.

In this sleeping hour,
With blankets around drowsy, dreaming lovers
And gentle rain against windows;
As wet earth's fragrance embraces the shining empty
streets and the gleaming trees,
My restless soul, this very strange and wandering soul
Cries out to you.
Will you awaken?
Will you open up your window to the wet and glittering night?
After the drenching rain cools your warm, beloved face,
If your eyes can see with mine
If your heart can sing with mine
If your mind can know with mine
I will have touched you.
I will have touched you, once again.

She didn't send it. Shaking her head, she slipped it into the notebook where she kept all the others.

Not many days later, she and Carlton found their way back to England, where the historical old village of Stratford-upon-Avon beckoned. The two arrived, theater tickets in hand, to absorb as much of Shakespeare's lore as might be possible in one day's time. Browsing the souvenir shops, skimming through volumes of the bard's sonnets, Elisabeth thought grimly about her own collection of verses.

I should trash all that stuff, once and for all.

But still she wrote her letters.

Tuesday

Dearest Jerry,

It is unusually warm—in the high 70s I'd guess. We saw *Richard II* this afternoon, performed by the Royal Shakespeare Company. How I love Shakespearian theater, and how rarely I've seen it performed well! At its best, it is truly one of my favorite things. Unfortunately, a migraine headache nearly ruined the thatched cottages for me—almost, but not quite.

I just realized why I've been feeling so sad. Things change so quickly here. Every day brings new sights, sounds, and faces. Are things different there as well? Surely you have forgotten me by now! I feel so very far away from you. I hope once in a while you've wanted to pick up the phone to call me, just to say hello.

That would be nice to know.

Love always,
Betty

Stratford behind them, the Caseys' final stop was London, where they were warmly and genuinely welcomed by the expatriate Mandaleys—Javier and Irina. Elisabeth was altogether delighted to be reunited with her old friend. The two women spent hours catching up on news and then turned their attention to more personal matters.

"How are you and Carlton getting along, Betty?"

"Oh, just fine! You know, we never quarrel." She had no sooner said it, when Elisabeth suddenly recalled the explosive encounter at James' party. . . ." Or at least hardly ever. Carlton's certainly a good provider, of course, and I really have nothing to complain about. After all, nobody's perfect. Right?"

Irina nodded. "By the way, what's that medicine you've been taking?"

"Oh, it's just Valium. I've been a little tense, you know, but it's no big deal."

Irina frowned at her friend, a grim expression turning down the corners of her mouth.

"I worry about you sometimes, Betty. I really do."

"I'm fine, Irina. Honest."

"Well you certainly look wonderful! That sweater is just your color!"

Elisabeth glanced down at her mauve turtleneck and smiled. "Remember how Dorothy hated pink? She hated my poetry, too!"

The two women laughed a little too loudly, both grateful that the subject had been changed. "Dorothy is a fool!"

"I thought she was your friend!"

"She is my friend. But she's a fool anyway."

After dinner that evening, Javier went out to a rehearsal, and Irina and Carlton started reminiscing about old times. Feeling a little left out, and thinking they might want to talk privately, Elisabeth said good night and returned to the guest room. To her relief, the bright yellow *National Geographic* she'd "borrowed" from the hotel room was still in her bag.

She absently turned the pages, shuddering as she skipped over a rather horrific article about spiders, hoping to find something slightly less scientific to read.

She checked the index.

"Ethiopian Famine." Perfect. Just what I was looking for—a little light reading.

Elisabeth opened to a two-page photograph of a dying African infant. The naked baby girl was emaciated beyond belief. Flies swarmed around her eyes. And, to Elisabeth's great dismay, the child's body was covered in ugly, bloody sores.

"Six weeks old . . ." the caption read.

She could only stare. She slammed the magazine shut, then quickly opened it and stared again. Painfully, Elisabeth recalled holding healthy little Brooke, the green-garbed baby on the plane. The very same age, born to affluent, American parents, she had been a perfect specimen of human life.

But what about this?

Elisabeth's arms felt weak. Her stomach churned. The withered, dusty black body. The distorted, jutting ribs. The flies. Worst of all, those hideous sores—she could almost feel them eating away at her own flesh.

Unexplainably, a cry rose in her throat. Before she could stop herself, she spoke out, "God, please! Isn't there something I can do to help? I have so much. I want to do something!"

"What did you say?" Her husband's voice startled her. She hadn't heard him come up the stairs.

"Oh, Carlton! Look at this picture. It just breaks my heart."

Puffing on his pipe, Carlton's face was blank with incomprehension. "So? Babies die every day. You know that, don't you?" He dropped the magazine back into her lap. "Just be glad for what you have! Oh, that reminds me. I need to check on prices. I want to go on a safari next year."

"A safari? Where?"

"Africa, of course. Kenya. Where else?"

Friday

My dear friend,

I'm mailing this from Heathrow Airport, on my way home. I left London soaking in rain and am joyfully headed for California's sunshine once again.

Can you believe this? Carlton told me last night that he wants to go on a safari to Africa next year! Unbelievable! It seems to me that I've spent my entire life avoiding being shipped off to Africa for one reason or another. As far as I'm concerned, no one will ever get me there!

All that matters at the moment, however, is that I'll be back in L.A. early Thursday.

Will you be there waiting for me?

Love, and more love,
Betty

Two weeks after her return flight from London, Elisabeth sat fidgeting at a candlelit table in Newport Beach, studying and restudying her flawless, scarlet manicure, watching impatiently for the black Datsun that would soon bring Jerry to her side. After frantically trying to reach him for days, she had finally talked to him by phone, and they had agreed to have dinner while Carlton was directing a musical on location in Hawaii.

Just forty-five minutes earlier, driving down the Santa Ana Freeway toward the beach cities, Elisabeth had experienced a terrifying attack of shortness of breath, which had literally forced her off the road. The car had been swayed and shaken by every passing car as she sat huddled miserably in the driver's seat, panting into a crumpled brown paper bag. These days she always carried a bag with her for such emergencies.

"When you breathe your own carbon dioxide, it acts as a sort of tranquilizer," Dr. Milton Jacob, her Beverly Hills internist, had explained during a recent appointment.

"You see, when you hyperventilate, you think you aren't getting enough air, but you really are. You just need to relax and the sensation will stop. I see this kind of situation all the time, you know."

More and more disturbed by the unsettling symptoms that plagued her nearly all the time, Elisabeth had been troubled by the doctor's probing questions. "Are you experiencing a great deal of stress? Is your marriage troubled? Do you see a psychiatrist?"

She'd tried to direct his attention elsewhere. "Well, I've been traveling, and maybe jet lag has something to do with it. Plus, I was really ill when I was younger, Doctor, and I'm afraid my heart just isn't quite what it should be."

"Your heart has a small murmur, Elisabeth, but I see no signs of damage or disease. Your symptoms all indicate anxiety, and to some degree, hypochondria. That doesn't mean you aren't feeling badly. It just means there's no physiological cause. It's emotional, and that's why the Valium you're taking is helpful."

No matter how comforting Dr. Jacob's words might have been, hyperventilation and chest pressure continued to grip Elisabeth in a vice of terror. She tried to integrate her own analysis with the doctor's diagnosis.

Carlton is suffocating me, and my heart is breaking over Jerry.

Today, considering the fact that she hadn't seen Jerry for nearly two months, this freeway episode was understandable. Making her way back into the traffic, she asked herself the same questions for the hundredth time.

Does he still feel the same way as he did before I left? What if he's met another woman? What if his conscience is bothering him about Carlton? What if . . .

After bombarding Camp Pendleton with piles of blue transatlantic air letters, Elisabeth couldn't wait to see what Jerry would have to say about her correspondence. Perhaps a little overoptimistically, she'd wanted to make him feel as if he'd been with her on the journey abroad. Besides, she'd secretly been quite pleased with her descriptive prose. Had he enjoyed it? Since the moment her plane had touched down at Los Angeles International Airport, every memory of the British Isles had been eclipsed by her anticipation of seeing him. Anxieties persisted, but excitement reigned supreme.

Meanwhile, Jerry was driving far too fast, northbound on the 405 Freeway from Camp Pendleton. He was as anxious to see Betty as she was to see him, although his thoughts were in no way focused on her literary achievements.

Jerry was an emotional, obsessive soul and tended to overdo nearly everything he enjoyed—hence the ceaseless sexual pursuits that had filled the last few years of his life with exhilarating highs and lows. And, quite naturally, certain Marine Corps traditions had added the element of pride to the otherwise mildly pornographic picture of his leisure-time activities. Jerry was unquestionably successful in "scoring" with nearly every woman he approached. But, like most single men, he was at the same time hoping to come across a "special someone" in the copulation process. He even allowed himself the vague fantasy that he might eventually want to settle down and become a family man.

Speeding down the freeway in his Datsun, the wind in his hair, Jerry couldn't help but wonder—could Betty somehow turn out to be the right woman for him? Sure she was married, but that made her devotion to him all the more flattering. Unpleasant memories carried him back over the years to Bethany Baptist Church, when he and Betty had played their well-rehearsed piano-organ offertories every Sunday. He'd barely noticed her affection for him at the time, so preoccupied had he been with Brenda Williams.

Jerry had been as much in love with Brenda as any teenager inexperienced in matters of affection could possibly be. She had been everything to him, his whole world, and he had wanted her desperately. Not only did he long to satisfy his rather overwhelming sexual desires, but he honestly treasured her sweetness and wanted to please her in every way.

With rising anger that had never left him, Jerry remembered the night he'd gone to the front of the church to "accept Jesus." Despite Betty's unspoken cynicism (which, by the way, had been silently shared by a large number of adult observers), Jerry had been more sincere than not in his effort to settle his personal accounts with heaven.

Unfortunately, his willingness to "try God" had marked the beginning of insurmountable troubles for him and Brenda. And it had heralded the end of his openness toward all matters of a spiritual nature, henceforth and forevermore.

After an emotional evening, seeing Brenda's tear-filled

eyes glowing with love unlike any he'd witnessed before or since, Jerry had agreed to meet with Rev. Turner for a series of compulsory "discipleship" meetings. These would teach him the necessary Baptist doctrines, "ground him" in the Word, and culminate in his baptism by immersion. It was in the second or third meeting, Jerry could never remember, that their conversation had suddenly turned to the matter of adolescent carnality.

Rev. Turner, obviously uncomfortable with the subject, had simply asked, "I trust you and Brenda are keeping yourselves circumspect in your relationship?"

The entire congregation knew, of course, and had fully discussed the fact that Brenda and Jerry had been seen making out in virtually every hidden corner of the church grounds.

"What do you mean, sir?"

"I mean," Turner had avoided Jerry's eyes and cleared his throat authoritatively, "are you sexually pure?"

"Well . . . ," naively Jerry told the older man the truth. "I wish we could go to bed together, but Brenda wants to wait."

Rev. Turner had turned on the boy furiously. "What do you mean you wish you could go to bed together?"

"Well, that's just the way I feel. I love her so much . . ."

"That's not love, son, that's LUST! And our Lord clearly said that if you have lust in your heart, you've already committed sexual immorality. The state of your heart is full of SIN, Jerry Baldwin."

The pastor's rage had astonished Jerry. Why such a violent response to the truth? Then Rev. Turner had said something even more shocking.

"Give me your church key."

Jerry, being the organist, always kept a key to the sanctuary so he could practice on Saturdays.

"Sure, fine. But why do you want the key?"

"Because I will not have a fornicator sitting on the organ bench in my church! When you've repented, and I see no signs of repentance at the moment, you let me know and we'll see about giving the key back to you."

Jerry had been overwhelmed with shame at first, and then confusion. He loved Brenda too much to think of himself as a fornicator. Somehow, even in his most erotic fantasies, he'd always thought of Brenda as a part of himself. Overcome by concupiscence though he often was, Jerry believed his feelings reflected more than simple sin.

But, in Jerry's quick mind, Rev. Turner's harsh words soon led to their necessary conclusion. If he and Brenda had already committed fornication by thinking about it, why put off the real thing a second longer?

Jerry had pleaded his case with Brenda, promising marriage, pledging eternal loyalty. He had spoken so eloquently that she'd submitted to his fervency. And the intimate time they'd spent together, both of them first-time lovers, had been tender and amazingly satisfying. The experience was repeated as often as possible.

Then Brenda missed her next period.

Once her plight was medically confirmed, Brenda's parents had alerted the church—a church Jerry hadn't set foot in since his ill-fated meeting with the pastor. The Williamses had been crisply advised to take their disgraced daughter to another town, to see her through the shameful pregnancy there, and to give the infant up for adoption. When they returned, it would be as if nothing had happened. Nothing at all.

The Williams family never returned. Brenda never saw Jerry again. And Jerry never forgave Bethany Baptist Church, Rev. Orville P. Turner, or the God of the universe for robbing him of the girl of his dreams.

Since that heartbreak, Jerry had been on a ceaseless quest to enjoy women in every possible way—without involving his heart. But now, after experiencing Betty's outpouring of impassioned writing from Europe, her beauty, and her adoration of him, he was on the verge of changing his approach. True, Jerry had barely read Betty's letters—he couldn't have cared less about landscapes and cities across the sea. But he'd hungrily devoured the emotion they contained.

The fact was, Jerry felt more like the man he'd always wanted to be when he viewed himself through Betty Fuller's/Elisabeth Casey's worshipful eyes.

And so it was, as he drove toward their long-awaited rendezvous, that Jerry was seriously considering adding the unfamiliar component of permanence to his relationship with Betty. First, he reasoned, they would make love. This would be no challenge, because he was clearly irresistible to her. Once he'd assured himself that she was as satisfying as he had so thoroughly imagined, the next step just might possibly involve his heart, not only his libido.

He drove into the Seashell Cafe parking lot, left his car unlocked, and bounded toward the door, filled with anticipation. When, at last, he appeared in Betty's view, he looked tanned and somehow more handsome than ever.

"Jerry!"

She stood up. His embrace was strong as ever, his gaze fixed upon her. "You look beautiful, Betty. I just can't take my eyes off your face."

Flustered and slightly embarrassed, she quickly changed the subject. "Did you get my letters?"

"Oh, yes, of course . . ." He smiled and took her hand across the table. "Look at me."

Elisabeth avoided his stare and instinctively scanned the patio and sidewalk, just in case some unexpected acquaintance might be watching. It was Newport Beach, yes, but people like James Novack weren't all that far away in Laguna, and the Seashell Cafe was a popular spot.

"Did you like my word pictures? I hope you feel like you went with me!" She didn't mean to ask for compliments, but longed to hear what he would say.

"I like *you*—that's what I like! Listen, Betty, I haven't seen you for a long time, and I want to be alone with you, somewhere we can talk. Are you really hungry?"

Fleetingly disappointed that there was to be no discussion of her poetic endeavors, she brushed away the sudden thought that Jerry just might not have read her letters at all. She was momentarily horrified that she had mailed all her memories away to someone who didn't care about them. Could it be?

Come to think of it, over the past months, Jerry had never really asked her much about herself at all. It had seemed all right, however, because he was otherwise so attentive. Clearly, he preferred to focus his attention on their mutual fascination with each other.

In any case, her stomach was in knots. She was dreading the decision of what to order, because she knew she'd end up pushing it around her plate with a fork anyway. "No, I'm really not all that hungry, Jerry. Where do you want to go?"

"Didn't you say your husband's out of town?"

"Yes, he's in Hawaii, working."

"How long will he be gone?"

"Till tomorrow night."

Jerry looked at her, his eyes warm with longing. Finally he said, "Why don't you show me where you live? I want to know what your home is like. Then, when we're apart, I can picture you there."

At first it seemed like a harmless idea to Betty. Then an electric current of excitement chased through her, feeling almost like fear.

What does he have in mind? Out of nowhere, she remembered his relationship with Brenda and its sad outcome. Lucilla had been quite pleased to fill her in on all the details. Was Jerry still as passionate as ever? She glanced a little shyly at him, contemplating a time of private affection. As she naively envisioned an hour or two of sweet words and soft kisses, Betty was more flattered than afraid.

"It's an hour away, Jerry. Are you sure?"

Jerry chuckled and winked at her. "I enjoy driving."

Again that electric current. "Are you *sure?*"

He laughed out loud. "Let's go, Betty."

At around 8:30 in the evening, Elisabeth nervously unlocked the front door of Carlton's enchanted cottage. Jerry had walked down the steps with her, his arm around her waist. He was still staring at her, hardly noticing anything else around him. Despite the fact that she was flattered, something seemed strangely uncomfortable. Was it guilt? Carlton was always pleased when other men paid attention to her. She doubted that he would mind if she entertained an old friend.

She quickly lit a fire in the fireplace and sank into the couch, then abruptly jumped up again. "Do you want some music?"

"Betty, come here beside me." Jerry's voice was husky and firm.

She seated herself next to him, feeling awkward and unexplainably ridiculous. "So what did you do while I was gone?" She was talking too fast and knew it. "Did the band perform anywhere?"

There was to be no answer to her inquiry. Jerry reached for her, and the passion with which he grasped her was a little frightening. She had never experienced such a response from a man. His hands moved warmly across her body toward the buttons on her blouse.

What on earth . . . this isn't what I wanted!

Her body viscerally responded, and she kissed him back. Her emotions warmed to the moment, and she tried to savor it. Ah, but her mind was stubborn and cold. Reason and right-eousness chilled her. She had to stop this before it was too late. What could she do? She wouldn't hurt him for the world, and she'd heard enough from Carmen and Leah about male egos to know that rejection at this point might well shatter their relationship.

This isn't what I wanted! The words thundered in her mind.

Elisabeth reached for her blouse and tried to laugh lightly. "Wait a minute, Jerry. Wouldn't it be more romantic with a little music playing?"

"Forget the music! You know this is what you've been wanting! Come on, Betty, let yourself go. It's going to be wonderful."

This isn't what I wanted. Elisabeth felt like screaming. Her mind raced. Jerry was fumbling with her blouse buttons again. Now he was unfastening his belt. Her physical excitement was all but gone, and from some dismal cavern of memory, one of Harold M. Fuller's unforgettable maxims echoed: "ALL MEN ARE ANIMALS! DON'T LET THEM FOOL YOU."

"Jerry!" She gently pushed his face away. "This isn't what I want. Not now. I love you, but I just can't . . ."

"Look, baby, I'm not known for my self-control, okay? I'm a Marine, remember? Besides, don't kid yourself. This *is* what you want. It's what every woman wants."

Jerry held her upper arms in his hands for a moment and studied her face, his eyes glazed with desire. "This is exactly what you want, and you're gonna get it."

"Jerry . . . wait a minute . . ." He muffled her words with his lips and tongue.

God help me. This is NOT what I wanted.

The phone rang.

She leaped to her feet, automatically straightening her clothes, forever grateful for the interruption.

"Carlton!" Never before in her life had she sounded so glad to hear from him. "You're where? What are you doing at the airport! Well I'm glad you called! I . . . I'll get the house cleaned up a bit before you get here. See you in a half-hour!"

At first, Jerry's frosty and frustrated departure hardly disturbed Elisabeth. She was unbelievably glad to see him go, incredibly relieved that she had escaped his intentions. She quickly set the house in order, carefully straightening up the sofa, thanking heaven for her timely deliverance. Then, as minutes ticked into hours, a heartache began to throb inside her.

Had Jerry been right? Had she deceived herself to think that she'd really wanted friendship and affection and communication? Had she actually been craving sex? She'd always felt very much in touch with her own feelings. Was she really so blind about this? The trip, for example. She'd really wanted to share every castle, every lake, every landscape with him. She wasn't inviting him to bed at all.

Was she?

She shook her head in disbelief. Humiliation washed over her in sad, tearful waves.

You asked for it, you stupid fool. All those phone calls. All those letters. What was he supposed to think?

Leah's bitter words replayed in her head . . . "Fact is, they're all alike. We want them to cherish us, admire us, pamper us, whatever. And what do they want? To get us into bed, of course. The rest is just formality!"

It hadn't applied to Carlton. But maybe his very unresponsiveness had somehow brought her to an unforeseen point of desperation. Jerry had said all the words Carlton never said. He had reached out in affection—if that's what it had been—the way Carlton never would. As a result, longing had sprouted in her heart, imperceptibly at first, and by the time she'd become aware of its growth, she'd almost succumbed to its strangulation.

What did I do wrong? Do men think I'm cheap? Do I come off like a whore? What happened? When did I go too far?

"Women are emotional. Men are sexual." She'd heard it somewhere, and surely not from Lucilla! But what did it mean? That apart from marriage, men and women were destined to have unaffectionate, superficial relationships? That men and women simply could not find a common ground in intimacy without getting between the proverbial sheets? That men would forever be knocking on bedroom doors, and women forever weeping at their lack of sensitivity?

It occurred to her that throughout her years of skin disease she'd been free to express interest and warmth, to be aggressively friendly to men as well as women. She'd used her intellect. She'd used her humor. She'd used her writing. She'd used her sincere interest in personal feelings. These had all been necessary tools for disarming people who were initially put off by her disfigurement.

Sure, she'd daydreamed about romance. But it all had been so safe. Males didn't respond to her sensually when she was trapped in a diseased body. Besides, to her remembrance, the deepest desire she'd consciously felt had been for the safety of warm and loving arms—a haven she'd never known, not even as a child.

But now she was faced with a dreadful dilemma. It was quite evident that her relationship with Carlton simply wasn't satisfying. Even the silly Neil Diamond incident had made that point. Perhaps her husband was unable, not unwilling, to meet her needs. So would she forever be looking outside her marriage for gratification of some sort? She thought about Carlton's disinterest. His distance. His unresponsiveness. She'd tried to communicate her concerns, and she knew that all the talk in the world wouldn't change him.

Why did he marry me in the first place? I really don't know. I just know one thing—he doesn't love me, and I don't love him. That's about all there is to it.

Elisabeth had plenty of time to puzzle over both age-old mysteries and present dilemmas. Carlton decided to stop at a friend's home in West Hollywood on his way home from the airport. Finally arriving at 2:00 A.M., after glancing at the mail piled on the desk, he climbed into bed beside sleepless Elisabeth.

"How many times have I told you not to leave that green book out on the coffee table?"

"That's my Richard Halliburton book, Carlton. It's my favorite book."

"I know. But it's green. The room is blue and red, right?" The sarcasm in his voice was edged with ice. "I know that doesn't mean anything to *you*, but it matters a great deal to *me*. Keep the green book in the chest after this. It doesn't belong on the coffee table."

Elisabeth got up and moved the book. Her heart racing, her breath unsatisfying to her lungs, she doubled up with stomach cramps and nausea and stumbled into the bathroom. She took two Valium. By 3:00 her churning stomach was quieted, but sleep eluded her still.

She tossed and turned. She felt as if she were collapsing from within, somehow folding in upon herself. At last, sensing the brink of insanity nearby, she cried out silently, frantically.

God, are you here? You've got to help me. I'm sick again, only this time it's on the inside. I'm confused and scared and ashamed. Are you here? Help me, God. I've ruined my life. I've got no hope for tomorrow. I've got no future, and I'm sick God, really, really sick.

Please help me.

Help me . . .

Help me.

Before dawn, Elisabeth awoke, wide-eyed and alert. She was cozy beneath blankets, but instantly aware of some other, deeper warmth heating her face.

What had awakened her? She looked around the room and saw only shadows cast by moonlight from beyond the leaded windows. No wind stirred in the trees outside. Only the steady sound of Carlton's breathing disturbed the silence.

Then, all at once, in the depths of her mind, she began to hear a message, a discourse composed of ancient words that had been penned by Hebrew prophets and poets thousands of years before. Had she learned them as a child or heard them in some long-forgotten church service? Where were they coming from?

No matter. The words were a response to her desperate appeal for help and read like a covenant between an unseen Father and His frightened child, rolling across the centuries.

I have loved you with an everlasting love, and so with loving kindness have I drawn you.

155

I know the plans I have for you, plans for welfare and not for calamity, to give you a future and a hope.

Fear not, for I am with you.

I will never leave you or forsake you.

Elisabeth bolted upright in bed. Her cheeks burned. Her heart hammered. Yet some strange peacefulness had thoroughly removed her fears. What had happened? Some sort of a flashback to her Sunday school days? When had she memorized all those verses?

Carlton stirred, opening one eye and looking in her direction. "What are you doing? Your face is all glittery," he mumbled and then rolled over again.

"Go back to sleep, Carlton. You're dreaming."

Elisabeth ran toward the bathroom, turned on the light, and studied her face. It seemed untouched by angel hands, so far as she could see.

Angels? Am I out of my mind? It's the stress. I'm having a nervous breakdown . . .

But then again, there was that peculiar peacefulness.

A bottle of Valium sat on the counter, its lid off. It was a new prescription from her doctor, and she'd only taken ten of the fifty white pills.

She stared at herself in the bathroom mirror, demanding reason of herself. She'd heard words in her mind before. They'd always been true. And this time she'd been awakened out of sound sleep to listen.

I'm either a psychotic atheist, or God is trying to tell me something. I think I'd rather believe the latter . . .

"God, is that You? Did you just tell me that You love me and You want to help me?" She whispered the question, and only the new tranquility within her heart replied. "Okay, God, if You're going to handle my problem, I won't be needing these . . ."

She flushed the pills down the toilet and threw the container in the trash. It seemed wasteful, but if God really was trying to help her, she had to show Him she believed Him and that she meant business. Walking back to her bed, she saw Carlton, slumbering peacefully there, oblivious to her situation.

She sat on the edge of the couch, where just the night before her own human needs had nearly seduced her.

"God, what would happen to me if I left Carlton?" The stigma of marital failure was not to be taken lightly, and even if God's grace remained intact, human reactions could be devastating. Lucilla had cancer. Would her only daughter's divorce accelerate her illness? In spite of herself, Elisabeth almost smiled. Blustering and rosy with rage, Harold would doubtless visit her again, bearing tidings of permanent parental estrangement. This time he would probably mean it.

Then, uninvited, the thought of James Novack's Laguna house drifted through her mind. It was a trivial matter, to be sure, and not really worthy of consideration. But it represented a dream come true, an important restoration of her lost girlhood. If she left Carlton, the house and the tower at Victoria Beach would certainly be lost forever.

Most critical of all was her own fate. Where would she live? Would she be able to support herself? Could she endure the rest of her life with the red badge "divorced" attached to her name? She wasn't exactly planning to spend her spare time at Bethany Baptist or any place remotely similar, but disgrace was disgrace.

After all was said and done, she knew that if she stayed with Carlton, she'd end up in an extramarital relationship sooner or later. On the other hand, if she left him and remarried, she'd be viewed as an adulteress anyway by much of the religious community.

Damned if I do, damned if I don't. The fact is, I can't stand it here. It's killing me. I've got to get out.

She sighed, put her head in her hands, and wept.

She was crushingly conscious of personal failure and frailty. She was unavoidably aware that Elisabeth Casey was a foolish woman whose future could only be salvaged by a miracle. But in that moment of absolute collapse, of personal devastation, of abandonment of self, something else happened. A safe, strong embrace she'd longed for all her life quietly and tenderly enveloped her.

Perhaps she knew.

Perhaps she didn't.

9

Elisabeth squealed the tires on her blue Fiat convertible as she pulled out of the stucco condominium complex and sped along Marengo Avenue toward the Pasadena Freeway. She had just moved the last of her belongings out of Carlton's Hollywood Hills cottage and was rushing through an October downpour to Bullock's Wilshire. Carlton had been out of town for two days, and she had decided to remove herself from his home while he wasn't around, avoiding any possible confrontation. She squinted at the roadway. The windshield wipers on the old Fiat were doing a pitiful job of clearing the water away.

At least it still runs! Elisabeth had hardly driven her car since her wedding. It had been stored in the garage because Carlton hadn't really liked the looks of it, preferring that his wife be seen in the white Jaguar. *Thank God we never sold it. The title is still in my name.*

Leah had helped her into the wee hours of the morning, and apart from a few last-minute items to be transported this morning, the job was done. She sighed with relief as her mind recounted a series of recent events.

It had been six weeks since her aborted rendezvous with
Jerry Baldwin and her subsequent encounter with the Almighty.
The following morning she had somehow managed to drag her
drained and disoriented body into work. She had spared everyone the details of Jerry's overtures, simply explaining that she'd
reached the end of her marital rope. Her friends had firmly
supported her decision to leave Carlton.

"I know it's against your religion and all that, Elisabeth,"
Leah had reacted with strong words, "but he treats you like crap.
I've never seen a man more rude to his wife."

"I'm not worried about God. I know He'll take care of
me . . ." Elisabeth was still feebly trying to warm herself with
the tiny flame of faith that had been ignited in her heart the night
before. "I'm not really worried about God."

"Where will you live?" Julia chose a more practical subject.

"Worse than that," Elisabeth sadly answered, "where will I
work? As much as I love you all, I can't afford to stay here. No one
could survive on Bullock's pay! The fact is, I don't know what to
do. I just know that I don't want any money from Carlton. I don't
want his help at all. I just want out, period."

The room exploded with dismayed cries: "You're crazy!"
"He's loaded!" "For God's sake, take him to the cleaners!"

"No." Elisabeth was firm, and her words carried a finality
that permanently ended the debate over Carlton's financial responsibilities. "I will not take money from Carlton. If I do, I'll have
to be in touch with him for the rest of my days. If I wanted that,
I'd stay married to him."

"You need to talk to Mr. G., Elisabeth." Carmen was always
enthusiastic about interpersonal dramas. "Mr. G. knows all kinds
of people. Maybe he can help you."

Later that day, Julia quietly asked Elisabeth if she could buy
her a cup of coffee. "I want you to think about something," Julia
began. "I have an escrow closing on a property next week. The
money is going into a trust fund for my daughter anyway, and

I'd like to loan you, say, $10,000 for awhile. Maybe five years or so. You won't make it unless you buy yourself a condo or something, Elisabeth. You need to build up some equity."

Julia was fascinated by real estate and had made a small fortune in clever transactions. But it was her kindness that touched Elisabeth. "How will I ever pay you back?"

"If you invest in a property, you can refinance it in five years. It will have appreciated substantially, and you'll be on your feet by then."

"What if . . ." Fear wrestled with hope in Elisabeth's heart. "What if I can't pay you back?"

Momentarily, Julia wondered the same thing. Then she smiled. "You'll pay me back. I'm not going to worry about it. So why should you?"

Feeling like a riverboat gambler, Elisabeth accepted Julia's check the following week and quickly invested in a one-bedroom unit north of Colorado Boulevard in Pasadena—the beautiful City of Roses. Carmen had discreetly arranged for someone in the Bullock's Wilshire payroll department to lie about Elisabeth's income so she would qualify for the loan. Sure enough, it had worked.

Elisabeth had yet to say a word to her parents about her decision to leave Carlton. She would fill them in once all the details of her life were settled. That way, there would be no attempts to talk her out of anything.

She wiped the interior fog off the windshield with an old washcloth and turned the heater to defrost.

I wonder how old Jerry's doing.

Jerry had written her one tortuous epistle, pledging his eternal love and informing her that she had truly broken his heart once and for all. He also reported that he was being transferred to the East Coast.

She answered his letter with the only poem she was ever to send him.

Ever alert,
Ever aware
Of ugly sin,
Of warped, misshapen evil,
We bravely follow beauty
Into the very furnace of Hell.

You nearly fooled me
With those eyes of yours.

As one might expect, Jerry never wrote again.

As for Carlton, he had reacted in his usual sedate way to the news of his wife's departure. "Well, dear, if that's the way you want it, naturally there's not a thing I can do to stop you." He paused thoughtfully and then, with the utmost insincerity, went on, "Is there, in fact, anything I can do to persuade you to stay?"

"No, Carlton. It's really better just to get on with our lives."

He nodded. "You realize, of course, that I'll be contacting an attorney."

"You won't need an attorney, Carlton. I don't want a thing."

He looked at her skeptically as he mixed himself a drink. "Right, dear. We'll see what happens."

Elisabeth had also called both James Novack in Laguna and Irina Mandelay in London to let them know of her plans. Her words with James were the first she'd had since his party and her seemingly ill-advised conversation with his sister.

"You aren't mad at me are you, James?"

"Mad at you? Of course not! Why would I be mad at you!"

"Oh, Carlton thought I might have offended you by talking to your sister about prayer."

"That's why I introduced you to my sister, sweetheart. I knew you'd understand each other. By the way, she thinks you're marvelous. And I guess you heard about my house?"

"What about your house?"

"I sold it last week."

"Sold it! Oh, James, why?"

"Because I needed money! Why else!"

Once she'd absorbed that shock, she gave him her own startling information. "I'm divorcing Carlton, James."

"Well, it's about time."

She was all but speechless. "What do you mean?"

"You know exactly what I mean. Your marriage was a farce from day one. You don't need to explain a thing. I already understand."

As for Irina, she was saddened but also surprisingly unruffled by the call. "I just want to see you happy, Betty, love. You've already been through enough."

That afternoon, Elisabeth had an appointment with Mr. G. He'd been hearing for some time, from Carmen, a soap-opera-style account of events that were quickly transpiring in the Casey household. He ushered her unceremoniously into his extravagantly paneled office.

"What can I do for you?" Ever direct, he asked the question before either one of them sat down. Elisabeth liked Mr. G. in an odd sort of way. He didn't mess around. Well, not with business matters anyway.

"I need a better job. I can't survive here."

"You're sort of a religious girl, aren't you?"

"Well, no. Well, I'm . . . yeah, I guess so. Why?"

"I've got an in-law in Pasadena who runs a little missionary outfit of some kind. He told me a week or so ago he was looking for a writer. Can you write?"

"I can write anything, Mr. Goldfield."

"He's Jim Richards. Here's his number. Tell him I told you to give him a call. Tell him I said you were the best writer I've ever met."

"Excuse me, but aren't you sticking your neck out a bit? You've never seen a single word I've written!"

"Who cares?" He laughed with delight, thoroughly enjoying his relative omnipotence. Then he stood up and escorted her through the huge oak doors. "Good-bye, kid." He said, "Keep your chin up."

Just as she walked out the door of the president's office, Leah rushed up to her.

"Elisabeth, you have a phone call. I'm not sure, but I think it's your father."

"My father?" Instinctively, Elisabeth felt a wave of panic. He'd never called her at work in his life. Something had happened to Lucilla. She grasped the receiver, feeling the old dizziness, her heart racing, her palms sweaty.

"Hello? Daddy?"

"Betty, your Mother is in real bad shape." Harold's words were choked with fear, shaky with emotion. "The ambulance is coming right now. She fell down, and now she can't talk right. Everything she says comes out in gibberish. I'm really afraid this is it . . ."

"I'll get myself up there as soon as I can get a flight. It sounds like she's had a stroke or something, doesn't it?"

"I don't know, Betty. I just don't know. Maybe it's the morphine or . . ."

"I'll let you know when I'm coming, Daddy. And I'll be praying. G'bye, Daddy. Bye."

Carmen had overheard the conversation. "Do you want a Valium, Elisabeth?"

There was no hesitation. "No, I don't. I'll be fine."

The Medford, Oregon hospital was like every other hospital Elisabeth had ever seen. Spotlessly clean. Glossy with pale green and cream enamel. And bustling with people—efficient medical personnel, diligent administrative workers, worried family members, and, of course, patients in varying degrees of misery.

On the way there, Harold had explained to his daughter for the umpteenth time that Lucilla wasn't making any sense and that the doctors didn't think she was aware of her aphasia. "She's just babbling away, and she's mad as a hornet because no one knows what she's saying!"

Sure enough, when Elisabeth entered the room, Lucilla's eyes brightened, she reached out a trembling hand, and a string of absolutely meaningless syllables came out of her mouth.

For several bizarre minutes, mother and daughter carried on a most peculiar conversation. Elisabeth pretended she understood every word, and her nods and "Yes, mother" responses encouraged Lucilla to even greater heights of communication.

"Sounds like she's speaking in tongues, don't it?" Harold's brother Simon guffawed. Simon and Elmer, Elisabeth's elderly fraternal uncles, had permanently entrenched themselves in Lucilla's room. The brothers rarely disagreed about anything, and naturally they shared their sister-in-law Lucilla's innate distaste for Pentecostalism.

Elisabeth frowned at Simon, not wanting her mother to hear him making light of her condition. Even though the poor woman couldn't speak, she could certainly hear. But, predictably, Simon was oblivious both to Lucilla's vulnerability and to Elisabeth's warning scowl.

"Yeah, somebody ought to tell her to lay off, all right. Everybody knows when you speak in tongues, there's got to be an interpreter present, and there ain't one here!" His laughter all but rocked the room.

You idiot. It's anything but funny.

"Shhh! You'll upset her." The forbidden subject of speaking in tongues had already caused Elisabeth enough stress to last a lifetime. She most assuredly did not want to introduce it into her mother's final thoughts.

At that point, Lucilla's oncologist appeared, and Elisabeth asked to speak with him privately.

"What's happened, Doctor?"

"Her initial tumor has metastasized to her brain and has caused a stroke. We expect more strokes at any moment because of the location of the tumor. If I were you, I would say good-bye to your mother."

"Can anything be done?"

"She never wanted us to take heroic steps once she reached the end. She's always been very adamant about it. Anything we could do now in terms of either radiation therapy or chemo-therapy might prolong her life, but the quality of life would be unacceptable. It's best you say good-bye. I doubt if you'll see her alive again."

That night, Elisabeth lay staring at the ceiling of her parents' guest room bed. Sleep was impossible, for she was examining an invisible but persistent portrait of her mother, curled in her hospital bed like a withered autumn leaf, her personal dignity lost in a steady stream of senseless babbling.

How could God let that happen to her? She must be so humiliated.

Elisabeth would never forget the rage with which Lucilla had attacked men and women who spoke in tongues. How odd. How very odd.

Did she have to be reduced to the very thing she's always hated?

Is death just a final deterioration of all we hold dear?

Does God have to break our pride on every level before we can look Him in the eye, face to face?

As sorrowful questions swarmed in her restless mind, Elisabeth heard the phone ring. Harold's muffled voice spoke to someone only briefly before his footsteps were moving closer. She glanced at the clock. It was 1:00 A.M.

"Betty?" he tapped softly on her door. There were tears in his voice.

"I'm awake Daddy. Come on in. What's happened?"

"She's gone. Went in her sleep. She's gone, Betty. Gone. What am I gonna do now?"

Apart from her pity for Harold, she was strangely unmoved by Lucilla's death. It had been looming for months, causing most of Elisabeth's grieving to be private and protracted. Now it was over, and the finality of Lucilla's departure was underscored by Harold's insistence that she "visit" her mother's open casket. It was a tradition that Elisabeth secretly despised.

When people are dead, they are DEAD. What's to look at?

The woman who lay in the satin-lined box was no one Elisabeth knew. The expression some embalmer had carefully frozen upon Lucilla's face had certainly never been there before. Only her hands seemed familiar.

Those are the hands that changed my diapers when I was a baby . . .

That thought recurred in Elisabeth's mind again and again during the brief visit to the Medford Mortuary. It was the only link with the past she could find. Perhaps infancy had been the one time when Lucilla had wholeheartedly loved her.

There would be no better time to assume so than now.

The funeral was a rural affair, graced by a closed casket, thanks to Elisabeth's stubborn insistence, and attended by more than a hundred of Lucilla's faithful Bible students. The sick woman had stoically taught a Bible class up until just a few months before, and she had been providing scriptural guidance by phone right up until her first stroke, just days before.

Three of Lucilla's favorite hymns were sung by a women's trio, accompanied by a somewhat inaccurate and teary-eyed pianist. The woman's grief evidently prevented her from reading the musical notes with even a modicum of precision. The result was a musical disaster.

After the pastor concluded the service by thanking God for Lucilla Fuller one last time, a Baptist potluck provided its own conclusive solace. In the church social hall a coffee pot perked fragrantly and mountains of food miraculously appeared, more food than could possibly have been consumed by twice the people present. Harold took home dozens of Tupperware containers, all destined for his freezer. The widower might not be ready to cope with life without his spouse, but at least he wouldn't starve to death.

The following day, a teary Harold drove Elisabeth to the airport. "Daddy . . ." She wasn't sure if it was a good time to tell him, but maybe his grief would insulate him from the shock.

"Daddy, I don't think Carlton and I are going to be married much longer . . ."

"What do you mean?"

"I'm pretty sure I'm going to leave him," she said, picturing her new condominium in her mind and wondering how long before she should give her father the address and phone number.

"I'm not surprised, Betty. He always seemed like a queer to me."

"Oh, Daddy, that's not it! I don't have any reason to think he's a . . . a homosexual. I just don't love him. That's all there is to it. I made a mistake, and I'm going to have to deal with it. But I just can't live with him anymore. It's too . . . well, uncomfortable."

"Your mother was worried about you, you know. She couldn't see how you could stand Carlton." By now he was parking the Ford. "Well, here we are. Let me know what you decide, Betty."

"I've pretty well decided, Daddy."

"Well, whatever you do, don't get yourself pregnant! You'll never be able to leave him if you're stuck with his kid."

"Daddy, believe me, that is no problem. Carlton and I haven't had a thing to do with each other for ages. Getting pregnant is the least of my worries and has been for a long time."

"Nobody else in the picture?"

"Nobody else."

"Well, like I said. I'm not surprised." They stood together at the United Airlines gate. Her flight to L.A. was boarding.

"What are you going to do, Daddy?"

The old man's eyes welled up. He was nearly seventy-five years old, and the future stretched before him, endless and empty without his beloved Lucilla. "I don't know, but I'll stick around here for awhile. No place else to go."

"I love you, Daddy."

He shook his head sadly, a mournful expression on his face. "I haven't been much of a father to you, Betty."

She was taken off guard. "Oh, Daddy," she responded

quietly. "I always knew you loved me."

"Well, I always did. I didn't say it and I didn't show it, but I always did love you."

Betty could see that Harold was close to losing control emotionally. She hugged him and kissed him on the cheek. "Don't worry. Everything's going to be fine. But I've got to go or I'll miss my flight."

"Okay. I gotta go too. Call me if you need anything. Take care of yourself, Betty. See you later."

Harold M. Fuller hugged his daughter firmly, then walked away without once looking back.

How many times in my life has he just turned his back and left me standing there, watching him go? Unexpected, sorrowful thoughts swept over Elisabeth. She had always wanted a closer relationship with Harold. Now she suddenly recognized how remote he had always been. *If God is supposed to be some sort of heavenly father, no wonder I have such a hard time thinking He is always with me, always caring for me, always wanting to do something wonderful for me.*

Out of nowhere, an instructive idea burst into her awareness. "Forgive your father. He has no idea what he does to you."

As always, Elisabeth wondered whether she was hearing divine orders, listening to her own conscience, or becoming psychotic. Eschewing the possibility of insanity, she chose simple obedience. *I do forgive him. He always does his best.*

Struggling with her own heartaches, Elisabeth couldn't have imagined the turmoil in her father's soul as he headed for his car. She would have been amazed to learn that the old man was sadly regretting his performance as a parent.

"I never loved her enough," he chastised himself. "And now, whether she divorces that jerk or not, she sure as heck doesn't need me. I don't even know her anymore. I still remember how much she loved me when she was a little girl . . ."

Harold sat in his car and wept, not only over his lost wife, but over the daughter he was unable to hold close to his heart. He knew that somehow Lucilla had always come between them. Vaguely fearing Lucilla's jealousy, he had allowed the estrangement—even insisted that it be so.

And now, with Lucilla gone, he was hopelessly unequipped to bridge the gap between his only child and himself. It was too late. Betty had always been from a different world, and she was even more so now. What did he have to offer her?

He put the key in the ignition and backed up the car. *I'm alone, and that's all there is to it. Maybe things shouldn't be the way they are.* He wiped his red eyes and blew his nose loudly into a handkerchief before heading homeward. *But what could I have done differently anyway?*

Meanwhile, seated on the plane, Elisabeth wrote a short note to Harold. She mailed it as soon as she arrived in California.

Dear Daddy,
    Here's another poem for your collection. This one is just for you.

    You cannot fly,
    You cannot sing,
    Neither can laughter chase away your gathering cares,
    But love can mend
        Your broken wing,
        And there is healing in the shelter of my prayers.

    I love you very, very much,

                                Betty

The international headquarters of Outreach Unlimited Ministries was housed in a mini-mall on the east side of Pasadena. Jim Richards was the executive director and also the brother-in-law of Karl Goldfield, Bullock's Wilshire's Mr. G. In spite of Elisabeth's instinctive distaste for all things missionary in nature, she was not about to reject a job at this stage of the game.

"Well, young lady! You come to us very highly recommended. Karl seems to feel like the sky's the limit when it comes to your writing ability."

Karl Goldfield is a compulsive liar. No wonder he's so successful.

She made a quick assessment of Jim and decided she felt comfortable with him. He was around forty-five, his dark brown hair thinning slightly, his waistline just a bit expansive. But he had a nice smile and a ready laugh. Besides, from what she could see, he and his small staff were doing great things in famine relief and medical aid, both in Africa and in Southeast Asia.

"What kind of writing do you need?"

"Oh, all kinds of things. We publish a monthly newsletter for one thing, and we like to write it ourselves. Also, although a direct mail house designs our fund appeals, we like to provide our own copy. More importantly, however, we have a series of books in mind . . ."

"Books!"

"Now don't panic." Jim chuckled at her horrified face. "You don't have to write a book your first day on the job. Here's the situation. We have a very fine Christian photographer working with us, a man by the name of Jon Surrey-Dixon. He's done assignments for *National Geographic, Smithsonian, Life*—a real pro. But since he likes to donate part of each year to Christian service, he's agreed to put together some pictorial books about the areas of the world where our ministry is at work. We'll be needing some copy to accompany his shots."

"What parts of the world are you talking about?"

I don't think I want to hear this.

"We'll be doing our first book about the homeless children of East Africa."

Elisabeth nearly groaned out loud.

I knew it. I just knew it. "I've never been to Africa . . ."

"Don't worry! If Jon feels you need to go to Africa in order to do the job, we'll send you over. You wouldn't have to pay your own way. Anyway, there's plenty of time for you to learn all sorts of things before we get the books under way. But tell, me do you have any questions about us?"

I'm doomed. I'm going to end up in Africa. The handwriting is on the wall.

"Not really. I assume you're interdenominational?"

"Yes, most of us are involved in charismatic churches."

"Is that the same as Pentecostal?"

"Not exactly the same, although most of the people we work with in the Third World are Pentecostal."

Sorry, Mother. Over your dead body . . .

"Well, Elisabeth, considering your high recommendation from Karl and your fine Christian background, I'm sure we'd like to work with you if you're comfortable working with us."

She'd already calculated the salary in relationship to her condo payment, food, and utilities. It would suffice. She was fairly sure she could manage the writing assignments. And, apart from the clearly "Christian" surroundings, which she would cope with for the sake of employment, no other hesitations remained in Elisabeth's mind. She needed a job. This one had opened up almost miraculously and just in the nick of time. Maybe she was actually supposed to be here!

Only one more thing had to be clarified. "You know, Jim, I'm in the midst of a divorce. I don't want anyone in your ministry to be unaware of that in case it presents a problem."

"I have no trouble with it. We've had other divorced individuals working with us. Anyway, I already knew about your situation. Karl told me, although I'm sure he never imagined it would make any difference."

"Well, okay. I guess that's all I need to know. So when do I start?"

"Why don't you come with me right now and meet the *real* executive director of Outreach Unlimited. Everyone thinks I'm in charge here, but I'll show you who really runs the show."

With that, they walked into an office near the rear of the building. "Elisabeth, I'd like to introduce you to Joyce Jimenez. Joyce, this is Elisabeth Casey. She's going to be our new writer."

Elisabeth looked in amazement at the tiny, sixty-plus-year-old Hispanic woman who beamed at her from a wheelchair. Joyce extended a deformed hand and Elisabeth quickly took it in her own. Bright brown eyes sparkled at Elisabeth, and a pleasant smile never left Joyce's face.

"I suppose he told you I run the ministry?" Joyce looked at Jim suspiciously.

"Well . . . something like that," Elisabeth laughed at the two, who were obviously dear friends.

Jim excused himself to take a phone call, and Elisabeth was left with Joyce. They took a few minutes to acquaint themselves with each other. Joyce had suffered for more than thirty years with rheumatoid arthritis. "God hasn't healed me yet," she announced cheerfully, "but He just may one of these days!"

Elisabeth almost wanted to say something about her own healing, but didn't. Instead she commented, "I had some physical problems in my teens and twenties. But I've never had to live with the kind of pain I know you have."

"Pain is pain, dear. At least I was healthy when I was a teenager. How sad for you. Those are supposed to be fun years!"

Elisabeth smiled at the woman's cheerful reply. "I think I'm going to learn a lot from you. More than how to write newsletter copy!"

"We'll learn from each other. Imagine being a model! You've done things I can only dream about. You must have some wonderful stories to tell!"

Nothing you'd want to hear, Joyce. You'd be better off reading the National Enquirer.

"Have you just moved to Pasadena, Elisabeth? Where are you planning to go to church?"

Uh-oh. Here it comes.

"Um, I don't know much about the area. Where do you attend?"

"Oh, there's a terrific Christian Fellowship near my home.

We meet in an old shopping center on Foothill at about 10:30 Sunday mornings. Let me know if you want to come."

"An old shopping center?"

Joyce wrote an address on the back of an index card and gave it to Elisabeth, who deposited it in her purse. "So when do you start work?"

"Jim didn't really say. When do you want me?"

"Do you have to give notice at your job?"

"Not really. They already know I'm leaving."

"Then how about Monday morning at 9:30?"

"I'll see you then. And Joyce, I'm so glad I met you. I think we're going to be friends."

"So do I! I like you already, Elisabeth. Maybe I'll see you Sunday."

I doubt it. But stranger things have happened.

"Maybe so. Bye now."

Elisabeth had planned to sleep late on Sunday morning, but for some reason she woke up at the ungodly hour of 7:30. Her new home was situated in an unusually quiet condominium complex, and she couldn't blame anyone for her wakefulness.

Oh, great. Now I suppose God wants me to go to church.

The thought irritated her immensely. She hadn't been to church more than three times in three years, and she certainly hadn't missed it. She rolled over and put the pillow over her head, hoping to muffle some inaudible sound.

Look, God. I've paid my church dues, okay? I've already heard enough pointless sermons, listened to enough off-key solos, and dozed through enough church socials to last me a lifetime.

God apparently wasn't convinced. Elisabeth couldn't get back to sleep. Disgusted, she threw the covers back and sat on the edge of the bed.

Oh, all right. All right!

After a cup of strong coffee, she stood over the floor furnace to warm herself up and then climbed into the shower. Taking her own sweet time to put on her makeup, dry her hair, read the paper, and get dressed, Elisabeth relished every moment of solitude in her new home. She had not yet missed Carlton—never once. As far as she was concerned, she never would.

Going to church cast a certain dreary shadow across Elisabeth's otherwise blissful Sunday. Here she was, right in the middle of a divorce, starting a new job, and living in an altogether unfamiliar environment. The last thing she needed was an uncomfortable social experience. And, to her way of thinking, church was the most uncomfortable social experience on earth.

The abandoned shopping center where the Christian Fellowship met was most unimpressive. It was more an eyesore than a church, and the only reason she knew she'd come to the right place was because of the crowds of cars in the parking lot, nearly every one adorned with a Christian bumper sticker. "Christians Aren't Perfect, Just Forgiven." "Smile! God Loves You!" "Beam Me Up, Jesus."

God! I've got to get out of here.

Just as she was about to make her escape, she saw Joyce Jimenez. Worse yet, Joyce saw her and waved joyfully.

Now I'm trapped. Oh, God, why did you ever have to invent church?

Finally inside and seated next to Joyce's wheelchair, Elisabeth was able to see that this "fellowship" was unlike any church she'd ever attended before. At 10:30, a casually dressed group of musicians, some with very long hair, gathered at the front of the big, open room. They began to play guitars, bass, drums, and a synthesizer. Without a word of instruction, everyone began to sing along. The very first song softened Elisabeth's heart.

> I have loved you,
> With an everlasting love,
> And so, with loving kindness
> Have I drawn thee.

The words, to her amazement, were the same ones she'd heard in the depths of that terrible night not so very long ago, when comforting thoughts had spilled across her mind. She wanted to cry as the people sang the song again and again.

Similar songs followed, nearly every one a well-loved Scripture set to music. Not one familiar Baptist hymn was to be heard, and not a hymn book was to be found. Everyone knew the words and sang them with eyes closed.

Here and there, a man or woman lifted open hands upward. It appeared to be a spontaneous act, some personal statement of worship, not intended to impress others. No one but Elisabeth was looking around anyway.

In a quiet moment between songs, Elisabeth could hear a soft murmur of voices. The people around her seemed to be praying, although she couldn't understand their words. Some of them still reached heavenward with upraised arms.

Suddenly a man's strong, deep voice spoke out. He sounded a little too pompous for her taste. *Uh-oh. Another church voice.* For some reason, however, the essence of his words distracted her from her skepticism.

> I am here, in the midst of you, my children.
> I have come to take away your fears,
> I have come to heal your diseases.
> I am your Healer, and the One who works all things
> together for your good.
> I will transform the things you have feared the most
> into your greatest blessings.
> I will transform the things that have wounded you
> into your greatest strengths.
> I will use your hands, your feet, your ideas, and your
> words to do my works among the peoples of the earth.
> Go, in my name, my children,
> And I will surely go with you.
> I will never leave you or forsake you.

The words were received with expressions of "Thank you," or "Thanks, Lord," by everyone, but somehow Elisabeth felt they were especially appropriate to her. Was she being self-centered to think such a thing? She had stifled her tears successfully through twenty-five or thirty minutes of music. Now she quickly wiped her eyes with a tissue.

Just then a young man in jeans walked to the front of the church. "I'd like to respond to that word from the Lord right now. Some of you are here in need of healing. Let's get into groups of two or three and pray for each other."

Elisabeth turned to Joyce and started to ask, "Will someone pray for you?" Just then a woman approached them.

"Susie, how are you?"

"Not so good, Joyce. You knew I had a bleeding ulcer didn't you? Well I've got to have surgery on Tuesday, and I check into the hospital tomorrow for tests. I'm scared."

Joyce looked at Elisabeth and smiled. "Elisabeth, why don't you pray for Susie?"

Elisabeth was mortified. She had never prayed for a sick person in her life. She glanced around the room and saw people with their hands on each other, fervently interceding. She had two choices—either she could run out of the room in humiliation, or she could pray for Susie. All things considered, she began to pray.

"Lord," she said, her voice as steady as she could make it. "You've healed me, and I thank You for that. And I believe You want to do the same thing for Susie. I pray that when she goes in for her tests tomorrow, the doctors will be amazed to find nothing on the x-rays. I pray that You will heal her right now. I ask You to do this in Jesus' name."

After they sat down, the young man in jeans gave a message of encouragement. Elisabeth hardly heard anything he said. She was still shaking from the healing prayer, wondering why on earth she'd allowed herself to get into such an awkward position.

It's a good thing Mother wasn't here.

"I'm so glad you came, Elisabeth! Did you enjoy it?"

She was determined to hide her embarrassment. "Well, to tell you the truth, I'm not much of churchgoer, Joyce. This was so different, though." She quickly thought back over the singing, the words the man spoke, and the healing service.

"It's like God was sort of participating in the service."

"Well, of course He was!" Joyce laughed merrily.

Elisabeth laughed too, but without mirth. "Bye, Joyce."

God? At church? What an outrageous idea. I'll tell you one thing. I'm getting out of here!

And so she did.

Monday afternoon found Elisabeth sitting in her cubicle at Outreach Unlimited, poring over piles of printed information that was intended to educate her about the ministry's twenty-two-year history. She'd been reading newspaper and magazine articles, brochures, and newsletters since 9:30 that morning.

Starving children. Victims of famine and war. Disease-ravaged villages. Refugee camps. Although Outreach Unlimited had heroically stretched caring hands into countless devastating circumstances, it was obvious that their efforts were nothing more than a gentle mist moving across a parched desert.

"We can't do everything, but we can help just one person at a time . . ."

She'd noticed the founder's quote on several publications and could easily grasp its significance. In the face of so much tragedy, any other perspective would lead to despair. She thought of the sickness of mind, body, and soul in the lives of people she knew. The same principle applied. Yet one question nagged.

With all the hurting people in the world, why would God have chosen to heal me? What about Joyce? What about all the millions of others He doesn't help?

"Elisabeth!" Joyce Jimenez's voice carried across the office and sounded urgent. "Come quick!"

"What's wrong?" Elisabeth rushed into Joyce's office. Her new friend's brown eyes twinkled happily.

"Nothing's wrong! Nothing at all. Remember Susie? The girl with the ulcer you prayed for yesterday? Pick up the phone. She wants to talk to you."

"Hello, Susie? This is Elisabeth. How'd the tests go?"

"That's why I'm calling. There was no trace of my ulcer! I just wanted to thank you for praying for me."

"No trace?" Elisabeth was dumbfounded. During the prayer time, she'd believed momentarily that God might want to do something. But she never expected to hear that He'd totally heal Susie.

"No trace at all?"

"My doctor took three extra x-rays thinking he'd missed something. He called in both of his associates, and they took two additional views. There is simply no trace of my ulcer. I'm calling you from home. My surgery's been canceled! Thank you so much, Elisabeth. I don't even know you, but I feel as if we're friends."

"Don't thank me! Thank God. I wouldn't have even been at church yesterday if it hadn't been for Him. I'm as amazed as you are. I can't believe my ears."

After saying good-bye to Susie, Elisabeth stared at Joyce, stunned beyond words.

What is going on, anyway? This is weird stuff!

Joyce's phone rang. "Yes, she's right here. I'll send her in."

"Elisabeth, that was Jim. Jon Surrey-Dixon is in his office at the moment. He's the photographer you'll be working with later on this year. Jim wants you to come in and meet him."

Having no time to generate any substantial worries, she breezily walked into the crowded, cluttered office Jim called his own, and extended her hand to a slender, red-haired man who sat across the desk from her boss. In her warmest voice she introduced herself, "Hi, you must be Mr. Surrey-Dixon. I'm Elisabeth

Casey. It's good to meet you."

"The pleasure is mine, Elisabeth. And please call me Jon." The photographer's soft voice carried the trace of an accent. It reminded her of someone, but who? At the moment she couldn't quite recall.

"Elisabeth, won't you sit down?" Jim motioned toward another chair that was cluttered with books and papers. "Oh, sorry, let me move all that." He dumped the pile on the floor.

"How long have you been writing, Elisabeth?" Jon's eyes were pale blue, and they shone with intelligence.

"Well, for years, really."

He's a professional photographer and I'm not a professional writer. He's going to think I'm a fool if I tell him I've never really written anything but poetry. What am I going to do if he asks?

"What kind of writing do you enjoy most?"

"I'm sort of a poet at heart, I guess. I love to write descriptive passages, but my first love is poetry."

"Do you have any of your work here?"

"My poetry?"

"Yes, I'd like to see it."

I am in serious trouble here. No way is this man going to want to work with me. He's a professional. I'm a fraud. Oh God, what am I going to do?

"I guess I could mail you some things, if you like."

"Great! Here's my card. I'm on my way overseas at the moment; in fact I'll only be in California for three more hours. Send it to my home in New York. By the way, here are a few of my shots, if you'd like to see them."

I should have asked. Why didn't I ask?

"I'd love to."

She thumbed through the handsome leatherbound portfolio, immediately aware of his exceptional talent. She'd actually seen some of his photographs in the national magazines. This man had impacted the world with his art. How on earth could she be expected to work with him?

Thanks a lot, God.

Just then, as she turned a page in his book, her eyes blinked in amazement. An entire page contained shots of . . . "Victoria Beach? That's my beach . . . and my tower!"

"Your tower?" He laughed, warmly and spontaneously. "How on earth could it be *your* tower?"

This is a very strange situation. Very strange indeed.

"Oh, well, I've gone there all my life, since I was a young girl. I used to stay there, in the house. It's a long story, really."

"Well, we certainly have one thing in common. The Victoria Beach tower is one of my favorite California landmarks. I always try to photograph it whenever I have the opportunity."

He checked his watch. "Look, I'm sure there's more to this Laguna story, Elisabeth, and I'm dying to hear the rest. But I've got a plane to catch. Do send the poetry to me, won't you?"

He stood up, slung his flight bag over his shoulder and reached out to shake Elisabeth's hand. "By the way, if you've written anything about *your* tower, don't fail to include it. I'll be looking forward to hearing from you."

10

It was a damp, cold morning in Pasadena and Elisabeth could hardly keep her teeth from chattering as she got ready for work. On her way out the door, she stopped momentarily in front of a full-length mirror to make sure the heavy wool vest she'd just pulled on over her blouse looked businesslike enough for the office.

Who cares anyway? Outreach Unlimited isn't exactly the fashion capital of the world.

The woman that looked back at her was attractively attired in corduroy and plaid, but she no longer had the severe, stylized look of a model. More than six months had passed since Elisabeth's first day at Outreach Unlimited Ministries. In that time her divorce had been finalized. Fifty-dollar haircuts and twenty-five-dollar manicures had been suspended indefinitely. Most significantly, her inner turmoil had quieted at last—psychosomatic illness seemed as faraway as the glamorous, egocentric life she'd known before.

Longer hair brushed her shoulders. Her nails were short and coated only with clear polish, and she wore the London sapphire ring where her diamond solitaire and wedding band once had been. Deep charcoal eye shadow had been lightened to muted gray. The trademark red Chanel lipstick was gone forever. There were those who might have preferred this new, softer look. But curiously, Elisabeth herself was rather unaware of the changes in her appearance. The time she'd spent with the hardworking employees and volunteers at her job had made some deep inroads into her thinking.

Day after day she watched dedicated men and women working overtime without pay, setting their personal lives aside for one cause or another. No one seemed worried about looks or clothes or finances. For that matter, no one spent much time discussing theology. Meeting the needs of others was the priority, not the making of impressions. There were notable exceptions, of course. But despite the fact that some of her co-workers projected the dreaded "missionary" image Elisabeth still resolutely rejected, her respect for the overall effort was undiminished.

One day she'd watched little Joyce, in all her twisted pain, bent over in her wheelchair for hours while sorting donated clothing, folding it, and placing it in cartons.

"How can you keep up with this pace, Joyce? I'm practically dead from exhaustion!"

Joyce had giggled, "It's a trick of mine. I refuse to think about myself when I'm trying to accomplish something worthwhile."

"There are people who would say you don't look out for yourself very well."

Joyce had been serene and sincere in her response. "I don't have to. The Lord takes care of me."

Die to yourself. Die to yourself. They don't actually say it, but these people are starting to play like a broken record with their work habits.

One rather self-centered concern had troubled Elisabeth for months, although she'd mentioned it to no one. Half a year before, with grave misgivings, she had mailed twenty-five of her best poems to Jon Surrey-Dixon. She hadn't heard a word from him since.

The fact that he hadn't liked them enough to respond didn't surprise her in the least. But what impact would his disinterest have upon her employment? She had been hired, at least in part, to develop descriptive captions for his photographs of needy children. Eventually Jim Richards would have to call her into his office and tell her someone else would be doing the writing.

Her only question was why hadn't it happened by now?

Driving to work that February morning, Elisabeth mulled over the issue of the poems. She'd second-guessed her choice of verses a thousand times since they'd thudded through the Pasadena Post Office mail slot. Humiliation chilled her as she remembered some of the personal revelations Jon Surrey-Dixon had read and rejected.

Mother used to tell me, "Don't wear your heart on your sleeve." But did I listen? I'll bet he had a good laugh . . .

By the time she pulled into her parking place, she was thoroughly depressed and had decided to talk to Joyce about her problem next time an opportunity presented itself.

Perhaps because of the thick, patchy fog outside, she was the first one to arrive at the office. Elisabeth unlocked the door, flipped on the lights, and made her way to her cubicle. Her IBM Selectric typewriter was shrouded in plastic. Just as she was about to head for the lunchroom to prepare a morning pot of coffee for everyone, she noticed a small blue envelope on her desk. No, it wasn't an envelope, it was an air letter.

A pang of memory shot through her. *I can't believe I sent that stupid Jerry Baldwin all those letters about my European trip and he never read a word!*

She picked it up and noticed that it had been posted in late December from somewhere in Brazil. It was addressed to Elisabeth Casey c/o Outreach Unlimited. Trying not to rip the flimsy paper to shreds in her curiosity and impatience, she finally got it unstuck and open.

Dear Elisabeth,

I'm writing to you from a plane on my way to the Amazon where I have an assignment to photograph the tragic destruction of the rain forests there. I've been traveling almost continuously since the day we met, and I'm sure you have forgotten by now that you mailed me your beautiful poetry. You'll be glad to know I have your work with me at this moment, and want you to know that I think it is most extraordinary.

Truthfully I was moved to tears by a couple of your poems—it was almost as if I'd written them myself. Perhaps most important of all, I am genuinely excited about working with you on the Africa book. Your words and my photographs will work well together since we think in much the same way.

Whether Jim has filled you in, I'm not sure. But I'm planning to start working on the book in March, and I will be back in Pasadena February 26. Could we get together at that time, maybe for lunch?

Once again, thank you for sharing your writing with me. I couldn't have enjoyed it more!

Your friend,
Jon

P.S. Would you mind if I called you Betty?

Elisabeth sank into her chair in a daze. She read the letter over and over and over again. Then all at once she announced out loud, "February 26? *This* is February 26!"

"Elisabeth, are you talking to me?"

Joyce had just arrived and was wheeling herself toward her office.

"I said, this is February 26, isn't it?"

"That's what my calendar says. Why?"

Elisabeth walked into Joyce's office and handed her the air letter without a word.

After reading it, Joyce scrutinized her friend's bemused expression. "From what Jim told me, Jon liked more than your poetry. He said he'd never expected to find someone quite like you in a missionary organization."

Neither did I.

Elisabeth sat down and stared blankly at Joyce's desk. She shook her head sadly. "What difference does it make? You can't imagine how much trouble I've had with men, Joyce. I can hardly stand the thought of working closely with one."

Especially if I might kind of like him . . .

"What kind of trouble?"

"Every kind you can imagine. To be honest, I don't trust men, and I don't trust myself, either.

"Isn't it like everything else? Our emotions are nothing but shifting sand, and anything we try to build on them collapses. Faith is the only solid foundation for anything. You're right. You can't trust yourself, but you can sure trust God."

Wouldn't Leah and Carmen just love this?

"You always say that about everything!" Elisabeth chuckled at her friend's eternally cheerful outlook. At times Joyce's ideas sounded just a trifle simplistic, a little like the dogmas of a cockeyed optimist. This was particularly intriguing when one considered that she was imprisoned in a deformed body, condemned to a wheelchair.

Elisabeth hesitated before she asked the question that had troubled her since her first day of work. "Joyce, I don't know how to say this, but does it ever bother you that God . . . well, that he hasn't healed you?"

Joyce nodded soberly. "I think a lot of people wonder about that. Yeah, sometimes it bothers me a lot. But I've learned something. God wants us to be healthy and beautiful in every way. The problem is, sometimes our beauty or talent or self-reliance gets between us and Him. When that happens, you can be sure He'll let the physical body suffer so He can place His hands on the soul."

"I can't believe you'd ever let anything come between you and God."

"Nowadays I probably wouldn't. But you didn't know me before I got sick. I had my own financial management business. I was making a lot of money and nothing was going to stop me from being one of California's few female Hispanic millionaires. I was well on my way when the arthritis symptoms started, and the doctor told me to rest. I wouldn't. I was working eighteen-hour days, determined to achieve my goals." Smiling ruefully, she concluded, "As you can see, I never did!"

"So are you saying God punished you?"

"No! He did not! He just loved me enough to give me the kind of riches that will last forever."

The two women searched each other's faces. Joyce's eyes were red-rimmed, and a frown was etched on Elisabeth's forehead. Aware that there was nothing more to be said, Elisabeth directed the conversation back to her own dilemma.

"Look, Joyce, I want you to know something. It's not this Jon whatever-his-name-is I'm worried about. It's my attitude in general."

"Like I said, don't worry about it. Just trust the Lord. But remember—men get hurt by women just as often as women get hurt by men."

"They do? Well, I suppose they do."

"Of course they do. Why wouldn't they?"

"Okay. Okay. I get the picture. I need to stop thinking about myself. I need to keep my mind on others. I need to die to myself, etcetera, etcetera." She sighed in resignation.

"Look at it this way. Trust in the Lord with all your heart and stop trying to figure everything out for yourself."

"Is that supposed to be a Bible verse?"

"It's from the Joyce Jimenez translation . . ."

At 11:45, just as predicted, Jon Surrey-Dixon walked through the door with Jim Richards. He immediately found Elisabeth's office. "Hello! Did you get my letter? Are we going to lunch?"

"I just got your letter today. Sure. I'd love to go."

Twenty minutes later, the three of them were warming themselves beside the Hamburger Hamlet fireplace, talking in earnest about the Africa book and how it would be put together.

"Betty . . . do you mind if I call you Betty? I have a very pretentious Aunt Elisabeth . . ."

"Betty's fine, Jon."

"Betty, I think you're going to have to meet me in Uganda. There's no way you an do this book without visiting the orphanages and meeting the children. Could you get away in late April or early May?"

There was such a lilt in his voice that for one unbelievable split-second she almost wanted to go right then.

God! How could you do this to me?

"Well sure, Jon. As far as I can see April or May would be fine. Let's see now. What do I need to do in the meantime? I'll probably need to get some shots. And I'll need to read up a little about the areas we'll be visiting . . ." She was trying desperately to form coherent sentences. Her faculties were in utter disarray.

Jim seemed to sense her confusion. "Betty, I hope you're not worried about going to Africa. You're going to love it there. And once you meet those children, believe me, your life will never be the same."

Die to yourself. Die to yourself. I don't want to die. Isn't it about time I lived?

Jon nodded and smiled at Jim's words. "You'll feel like the most privileged person on earth when you see how difficult life can be for those kids and how absolutely joyful they are in spite of everything."

The conversation continued for another half-hour, when it came time for Jim to drive Jon back to the airport. Jon shook Elisabeth's hand and gave her a quick kiss on the cheek as they said their good-byes.

"It was great seeing you again, Betty. I'll try to call you in a week or so and give you some ideas I have for the book's format. Don't forget to get your shots! Next time I see you, it'll probably be at the Nile Grille in Kampala."

Leaving the parking lot, Elisabeth absently steered the Fiat right on Del Mar Avenue and headed east. Trying to distract herself, she turned on the radio. To her disbelief, a band called Toto was singing a popular song called "Africa." "I seek to cure what's deep inside . . ." Elisabeth clicked off the radio with a vengeance.

"Kilimanjaro. The Serengeti. *Africa!* Some cure! Oh, all right. All right! All right!" she shouted at the sky. She pounded on the steering wheel. She shook her fist in the face of heaven.

"You've won, haven't You? I'm going to Africa, and there's not a thing I can do about it. And if I could see You I *know* You'd be laughing! I just *know* it!"

Suddenly, and without warning, Elisabeth was laughing too.

A timeworn Uganda Airlines 707 droned unsteadily above the Sahara, its weary engines carrying a load of Ugandan nationals, a handful of Irish nuns, and an odd assortment of other Caucasians toward what Elisabeth had always thought of as "deepest, darkest Africa." The plane was untidy, smelly, and persistently emitted an endless assortment of unexplainable sounds. Again and again, Elisabeth was rocked by waves of terror, involuntarily envisioning the plane's burned wreckage being mournfully reported on the 11:00 L.A. news.

If the cabin looks like this, I can just imagine the condition of the engines.

Elisabeth's seat belt buckle was marked with a Pam Am logo. The one next to her said KLM. The "Fasten Seat belts, No Smoking" sign was in Arabic. Topping it all off, a most unpleasant odor had permeated the aircraft since takeoff from London-Gatwick. It was the first time in her life that Elisabeth had been grateful for the familiar scent of tobacco smoke that drifted throughout the cabin in dense, blue-gray clouds.

She had tried to sleep several times, but anxieties jolted her awake at the rate of six or seven worries per minute. Certainly Jim and Joyce had done everything imaginable to make her feel prepared for the journey. They had given her explicit instructions about how to get through customs and currency exchanges, who would pick her up, and what to say at military roadblocks.

Uganda had been locked in civil unrest for more than twenty years. The evil legacy of Idi Amin was well known to the Western world; less notorious but equally deadly had been Milton Obote, his dictatorial successor. Recorded deaths and atrocities had numbered in the millions. The true victims were the orphans, untold numbers of them, who had lost their parents to the frightful "armed men." These surviving boys and girls were the chief concern of Outreach Unlimited.

Now an altogether different government had taken power in Kampala, and a new leader was trying to piece together his beleaguered nation. Considering the state of affairs, he had his hands quite full.

Uganda had once been described by Winston Churchill as the Pearl of Africa. It had been a tourist paradise, an economic paragon, an educator's dream. The despotic regimes of Amin and Obote had done far more than create an environment where mass killing became an everyday affair. They had also destroyed the water system. They had allowed the roadways to become virtually impassable. Transport and communication systems had been rendered useless, except in the heart of Kampala, and there, like the Ugandan power company, they remained thoroughly undependable.

Because sanitation and water purification systems had been ravaged, disease had followed in the wake of the gunfire, and the dying had continued. Typhoid. Malaria. Yellow fever. Cholera. Life was dangerous, not only for those who lived in Uganda, but for anyone who chose to travel there.

Jon Surrey-Dixon had spoken to Elisabeth several times by phone over the past few weeks. He had offered his own words of encouragement and seemed to be genuinely looking forward to their meeting in Kampala.

"You needn't fret. I've been to East Africa seven or eight times, and I really do know my way around. You have nothing to worry about. Believe it or not, Betty, you'll love Uganda."

In the course of their conversations, she'd learned that Jon had been born and raised in Christchurch, New Zealand. He had begun his career there as a graphic artist, a field in which he still dabbled occasionally when he wasn't frantically traversing the globe.

Jon claimed to be devoted to English literature, classical music, and American football.

He'd explained his hyphenated name with a sweep of the hand, "I am the result of a rather ill-timed and poorly planned love affair, which caused my last name to become the subject of a great debate."

And when Elisabeth had asked him what church he attended he'd said, "I'm a cradle Roman Catholic with a lot of Pentecostal friends."

Sorry, Mother. It just couldn't be helped.

Probably because they provided him with a more-than-sufficient income, Jon was extremely interested in world affairs, but strictly from a human-interest perspective. He seemed to have visited every continent on earth, observing the faces of joy and sorrow, life and death through his well-worn viewfinder.

Elisabeth was fascinated by Jon, but had steadfastly refused to invest her time in pondering him. Only in quiet moments late at night, or when she heard his name, or when his memory unexpectedly drifted through her mind had she allowed herself to think of him.

But now she was beginning to wonder what the days to come might hold. In spite of herself, she began to envision conversations and walks with this new and exceptional man. She thought about what he would say to her. She tried to perfect her responses.

The truth of the matter was, she was going to meet Jon Surrey-Dixon in less than forty-eight hours. They'd only spoken face to face twice before. She couldn't wait to see him again.

Fighting off another bout of nervousness, she glanced around. There were several spinsterly Aunt Abigail types dozing here and there about the plane, each one traveling unaccompanied. Was she going to end up like that—dowdy and plain and alone? The nuns were somehow more appealing—they all had cheerful faces, and their single status was, at least, voluntary.

Aunt Abigail—she must be about a hundred years old by now, and I'll bet she's grouchier than ever. Maybe if I concentrate on Richard Halliburton instead of Aunt Abigail I'll be happier. I think I'd rather be an adventurer than a missionary.

Elisabeth's first glimpse of Africa came at daybreak. From twenty thousand feet above, she looked down in wonder upon the River Nile as it wended its lazy way through dense woods and broad stretches of brown terrain. Then, just before landing, she caught sight of the tranquil waters of Lake Victoria. From its forested shores, birds soared peacefully into a morning sky that was scattered with clouds. It was, undeniably, a breathtaking view.

What did I expect? Barbed wire?

Her appreciation of the quiet beauty was abruptly cut short as Elisabeth gratefully found herself disembarking the aircraft and entering the hustle and bustle of the Ugandan passport control and customs process. Fortunately, although the procedures took more than two hours, she was received into the country without incident. Her visa was examined, her passport was stamped, and soon thereafter she was intercepted by a woman who seemed to know her. She later learned that Rose, who worked in customs, had connections with Outreach Unlimited. Consequently Elisabeth's bags went through virtually unchecked. Next she traded two hundred dollars for a two-inch wad of shillings. Unfamiliar with the exchange rate, she could only hope the transaction had been fair.

At last she emerged from the airport into the sunlight, where she was immediately recognized and greeted by Josephine Muwanga, the Ministry's Ugandan director. A small, energetic woman, Josephine had a dazzling smile and a wonderfully warm personality. "You look just like your picture! But are you Elisabeth, or Betty? Which is it? One letter I received calls you Elisabeth and the other Betty."

With no more than a moment's hesitation, she replied, "You can call me Betty. That's fine."

"How was your flight?"

The most terrifying experience of my entire life.

"It was just fine. That's a rather old airplane, you know, but there was no problem."

"Oh, yes, it is *very* old. The children have been praying for you." The small Ugandan woman laughed mischievously. "Let's go see them!"

With that, the two women climbed into a battered, mud-streaked Land Rover, and the driver, a young man named Thomas, sent it roaring toward Kampala. They passed through the first roadblock between Entebbe and the capital city with no difficulty, thanks to Josephine's cheery dialogue with the surly, heavily armed soldiers.

Heaven only knows what she's telling them. I wish Jon were here.

The roadblock was located just past the old Entebbe airport terminal. In the distance, Elisabeth could see an Israeli jetliner lying in state, its paint faded by the years. It had remained a mute historical monument since June 1976 when the infamous Entebbe raid had taken place. Elisabeth racked her brain to remember the details of the story.

I'll have to ask Jon. He'll know.

Now camouflage-clad soldiers were everywhere, casually bearing automatic weapons almost as if they were toy guns. Somehow this widespread military presence was unalarming to Elisabeth. Instead, it was the unknown, the unfamiliar, the unpredictable that created all the tension in the pit of her stomach.

Fortunately, the second roadblock presented no more problems than the first, and before long the car arrived in one of Kampala's suburban villages, at the Bwayise Children's

Home. As if on cue, a half-dozen barefoot children opened the steel-and-wood gates, shyly looked into the car, and then ran to tell the others that the honored guest had arrived.

Once inside, Josephine introduced Elisabeth. "This is Auntie Betty, children. She has come from America to write a book about you!" When Josephine repeated the information in Lugandan, everyone applauded and cheered. Over the course of the next hour or two, "You are welcome" was whispered by nearly every adult and older child. The little ones simply extended their hands timidly and knelt.

"Betty, this will be your bed. I hope you don't mind sharing a room with Martha and Deborah. We're a little short of space."

"Of course I don't mind." Betty looked with astonishment at the clean bed next to the window.

Am I really here? Is that really my bed?

"Where shall I put my things?"

All at once Betty had four or five would-be servants, each one kneeling in traditional respect, helping with her clothes, bringing her tea, searching for a table for her toiletries, and presenting her with an electric kettle for boiling her drinking water—"twenty minutes and it will be fine."

A smoky scent lingered in the hot midday air. The day was on the verge of becoming unbearably hot and sticky. By 2:00, sweaty and stiff, Betty stretched out on her bed, her sleep-starved eyes beginning to close involuntarily. Just then a gentle breeze began to rustle the banana tree fronds outside her window. She glanced outside to see towering clouds piled up along the horizon, and she could hear the sound of distant thunder. Her apprehensions were fading. The unknown was here, all around her, and it seemed remarkably pleasant.

Jon will be here tomorrow. From then on, I'll have a friend to show me around.

Half an hour later, she sat on the edge of her bed, sipping hot, milky tea and thinking that Africa really wasn't so bad after all. Josephine pulled up a chair and joined her.

"Auntie, we have received word from Jon that he will be delayed by a week. Here is a letter for you."

Panic seized Elisabeth. She didn't know if she was more hurt or frightened. A week alone? She felt like bursting into tears. How could he be so inconsiderate?

Dear Betty,

I am so sorry we won't be able to meet on Thursday as originally planned. I have been sent on an emergency assignment to Cameroon and won't be able to make flight connections until next Tuesday. I wish I could be there to help you get acquainted with Uganda, but I suspect that Josephine is a better guide than I am anyway. In the meantime, will you try and get to know the children and find out a little about their personal histories? As I told you before, I'd like to focus the book on four or five of them.

I am almost certain I'll be there on Tuesday, and since you don't leave until the next Friday, we'll have a couple of full days to work together. I'm truly sorry about the delay, but it was unavoidable.

Your friend,
Jon

In the hours that followed, Betty napped, waking several times to the sound of children playing. Weary with jet lag, weak with disappointment, she felt as if she never wanted to wake up. When at last she did, a single thought emerged, clear and distinct from her own confusion.

Jon didn't send you here. I did.

The thought was both uncomplicated and transformative. If some unseen hand had transported her all the way to Uganda, surely her schedule would be planned in advance. Surely she'd be protected. Guided. In fact maybe—just maybe—Someone might even help her find some joy in what she was doing.

That afternoon she admiringly watched the gleaming, dark faces that surrounded her. Never had she seen such smiles.

Nowhere had she encountered such courtesy in children. As she reached out and pulled a beaming toddler into her lap, she suddenly remembered the *National Geographic* photograph of the dying Ethiopian infant. She recalled her cry, "Isn't there something I can do?"

And now here she was. Amazing. So what if she was faced with Jon's absence for several more days.

Who needs men?

Just then, out of nowhere, she recalled an absurd bit of Shakespearian commentary that she had apparently memorized in some long-forgotten English literature class.

> Sigh no more, ladies, sigh no more,
> Men were deceivers ever;
> One foot in sea, and one on shore,
> To one thing constant never.
> Then sigh not so
> But let them go,
> And be you blithe and bonny . . .

Blithe and bonny, indeed, you insensitive old bard! I suppose what you're really saying is "make the best of it." Well, that's exactly what I'm going to do. The fact is, I don't know whether Jon's a deceiver, or whether he's utterly inconstant. But he's sure had one foot in the sea and one on the shore as long as I've know him . . .

At last Tuesday arrived in Kampala, rain-splashed and cool, the air washed clean by a series of afternoon showers. Elisabeth found Jon at the Nile Grille, seated at one of the white-painted outdoor tables, drinking a soda, scribbling notes in a Daytimer. She was nearly an hour late and was relieved that he was still there.

"Jon!"

He stood up immediately, smiled in delight at seeing her, and hugged her enthusiastically.

"Jon, I'm so sorry I'm late! I got involved with some of the children, and by the time I was ready to come, I had to wait for Thomas to drop Josephine over at the market. I was afraid you'd think I hadn't got your message."

"You're sorry *you're* late? I'm a week late! How has it been? I'll bet you could have shot me when you heard I wasn't coming."

Her mind raced backward to the disappointment that had so devastated her just a week before. It seemed as if a lifetime had passed since she'd heard he wasn't coming. In all her remembrance, she'd never been happier than during the past seven days.

"Of course I wasn't exactly thrilled by the news, Jon, but to tell you the truth, I've had a fabulous time! If you'd been here, I'm not sure I would have had the chance to get to know the kids the way I have. We've spent every moment together. I've gone with them to the well, to the village, to their school, to their little Pentecostal church. We've peeled matoke, shopped for pineapples, cooked rice and beans, cleaned floors, carried water, fed chickens, tended the garden. Jon, if I were small and black, I'd feel like one of the gang! I've filled two whole notebooks with biographies and descriptions and little stories—even a few poems, Jon! It's been so wonderful!"

Her enthusiasm grew with every word, and she was surprised to see a look of sadness drift across Jon's face.

"Well, it sounds to me like I should have stayed in Cameroon."

"Jon, don't be silly! I'm really looking forward to having some time with you in the next couple of days. Unless, of course, you're flying to Saudi Arabia or somewhere tomorrow . . ."

"I'm here until Friday, Betty," he said quietly.

"Where are you staying, anyway?"

"At a guest house near Namirembe Cathedral. Have you had a chance to see the cathedral?"

"No. Is it worth seeing?"

"Why don't you decide for yourself?"

With that, they left the Nile Grille together, heading for Namirembe Hill.

The events of the following two days moved from one to the next in a kaleidoscope of images. Roadside villages. Lake Victoria shorelines. Highways pocked with massive potholes. Rusted-out military tanks. Skeletons piled along roadsides. Thatched huts. Bombed-out buildings. Soldiers and guns. Graceful women in colorful basutis. Men in proud white konzus. Sun-warmed days. Humid, star-strewn nights. And children—those beautiful Ugandan children.

"My only regret is that I'm not going to see Kilimanjaro," she told Jon during their last day together. "God and I have a private little joke about that mountain."

"Aren't you flying out through Kenya?"

"Yes, but I think Kilimanjaro is several hours from Nairobi and I've only got a twenty-four-hour layover."

"What airline?"

"I'm flying to London on British Airways. My Uganda Airlines flight was canceled."

"Lucky you."

"No kidding!"

And so it was that Betty's personal tour of Uganda came to an end. She had been escorted by the most delightful man she'd ever met in her whole life. She was forever amazed that, after all the years, such a remarkable person had entered her world, and it seemed entirely possible that he might stay there for a while. She admired him, enjoyed him, delighted in his company.

But dear as he was, she was determined to get on with her life, to live just as happily without him. The last thing Elisabeth Casey needed was another heartbreak.

They said farewell outside the Bwayise Children's Home, in the heat of a blistering afternoon, with a choir of birds caroling in the background. Smoke from countless charcoal cooking fires was already darkening the air. Jon was to leave Uganda the following morning; she, the following afternoon.

His palm was damp with sweat as he took her hand in his.

"Next time you come here, I'll be right here with you. No Cameroon detours, I promise."

"What do you mean, 'next time'? What makes you think I'll be back?"

"You won't be able to stay away. Africa gets in your blood. Haven't you noticed?"

She didn't answer. She was trying hard to fight unwelcome tears that were springing from somewhere deep in her heart.

"Why don't you go with me to Laguna Beach once I get back to California? You can show me *your* tower, and maybe if you're a good girl I'll take your picture in front of it."

"Okay, it's a deal." But for some reason, she didn't want to talk about going home right then. Hearing the children's voices, she glanced back toward the house. "Look, I promised some of the girls I'd go with them to get water. Then, after that, the rest of the kids are going to sing some songs for me. A little good-bye concert, I guess."

Again the tears. Where were they coming from?

"I'd better let you go, Betty. I'll see you in California."

"Good-bye, Jon."

He kissed her quickly and headed for the main road to find a cab.

Before sundown, she went with the children to the well. Once again, thunder was rumbling across the gray heavens, and as raindrops sprinkled against the soil, they brought forth a rich, earthy fragrance.

Together they walked down the rutted road one last time, each one carrying a colorful tub or a plastic jerry can. The fifteen-minute journey, made shorter by the singing of happy songs, ended at the "well," which amounted to four broken pipes spilling clear water into a muddy ditch. The children made their way down several stone steps, collected the precious water, then struggled to lift the heavy containers onto their heads.

Watching them fondly, and mentally saying farewell, Elisabeth remembered the texture of three-year-old Miriam's dark, curly head as she'd stroked it against her breast. She recalled a time when she had laid her palm upon little Katembe's fevered brow and had prayed, believing that his malaria would soon subside, rejoicing when it did. She thought back upon the touch of Sarah's small hand in hers, as the two of them ambled joyfully along a dusty road, talking about faraway places with strange-sounding names.

By the time they got back to the house and had sloshed all the water into a big aluminum tank, they were wet to the skin. What the spilling water hadn't dampened, the rain had soaked.

Betty went dripping into her room, searching for the already damp towel she'd been using all week. It was useless, considering the amount of water her clothes and hair had absorbed. How would she ever make herself presentable in time to hear the children sing? She was just about to plug in her hair dryer, praying that the electricity wouldn't black out until she finished, when she heard a knock on her door.

"Auntie Betty, a messenger has brought a letter for you. I believe it is from Uncle Jon."

Martha, a broadfaced girl with the gentlest of eyes, knelt courteously as she handed the envelope to her. The handwriting was familiar. A smile spontaneously spread across Elisabeth's face.

Betty,

I have an idea! If you'll extend your stay by two days, I'll hire a car and take you to Kilimanjaro. In any case, I've decided to fly out through Nairobi, so I'll meet your plane at the airport.

At least we can have dinner together. Will you indulge me and let me take you to the Norfolk Hotel? It's time you experienced a slightly different style of African dining.

See you tomorrow.

With love,
Jon

This is a surprise . . . this really surprises me . . .

Elisabeth read the letter four or five times before she suddenly became aware of the gracious young African woman who was still kneeling beside her. "Oh, thank you so much Martha. This is very good news—very good news indeed."

Hours later, deep in the African night a million crickets sang to the stars, and a full moon rose in tropical majesty. Drowsy but pensive, Elisabeth watched its slow progress, gazing through the tattered window screen and beyond the banana tree.

She heard Deborah and Martha snoring softly in the other beds, and in the distance the popcorn sound of an automatic weapon broke the stillness momentarily. A death? A warning? She'd heard the same sound nearly every night, sometimes closer, sometimes farther away. Whatever it meant to someone else, Elisabeth was safe and secure in the Bwayise Children's Home tonight.

And as for tomorrow?

Heaven only knows.

With that succinct response to her own question, Elisabeth Casey rolled over, swatted at a whining mosquito and fell asleep.

11

Gray and silver clouds hung low across the wide Kenyan sky. Although the air felt pleasantly warm and humid, the horizon was fully overcast. Unfortunately, so was Mount Kilimanjaro.

Only one more day here. I sure hope I get to see it.

Squinting out her window across parched plains, Elisabeth tried to force the mountain's outline to materialize. In the distance, she could see silhouettes of wind-sculpted, flat-topped trees. Legions of zebras and wildebeasts and even a small herd of elephants lifted columns of dust heavenward as they ambled along. But try as she might, Betty was unable to discern even the trace of Kilimanjaro. With a sigh, she turned back toward her simple, pleasant room. The Amboseli Safari Lodge featured varnished wooden walls and floors, bathrooms with running water, and clean beds canopied with glorious, ceiling-high mosquito nets.

The night before, she and Jon Surrey-Dixon had dined together at the Norfolk Hotel in Nairobi. Just as he had predicted, the fine cuisine was not at all reminiscent of the matoke and groundnut sauce offered at Bwayise Children's Home. Delectable seafood and fine cuts of meat had graced the menu, accompanied by all the right side dishes and beverages.

But it was the conversation and the company that Elisabeth had most enjoyed. She and Jon had talked and laughed into the wee hours of the morning—about Africa, America, and New Zealand, about poetry and photography, about mutual friends and life at Outreach Unlimited Ministries. They hadn't really delved into personal matters, and it wasn't Jon's words that lingered in her mind, anyway. It was, well, something else. Something she couldn't quite define. Even now, with him just a few feet away in the next lodge room, warmth flooded her as she thought about him, and tears burned her eyes once more.

It's just because I'm tired. I'm always weepy when I get too tired.

In actual fact, she was exhausted. She and Jon had left Nairobi for Amboseli before 8:00 A.M. To make matters worse, she had barely slept all night, her mind spinning and swirling with impressions of Jon's face, his words, and his laughter. They had driven for six hours, southeast toward the Tanzanian border, and the last two hours of the trip had been a dust-choked affair, their Isuzu Trooper bouncing wildly along the hard-packed, rutted dirt roadway. Jon had hired a driver, a Kenyan with the broad smile, who obviously believed that the rougher the road, the faster the vehicle should be driven.

Following that tortuous journey they had barely had time to deposit their belongings in their rooms before the driver insisted on taking them out for their first tour of Amboseli's watering holes, searching for "the big ones"—lions, black rhinos, hippopotamuses, and the like. How strange to see ostriches racing across open fields, vultures grimly stationed in odd-shaped trees, and water buffalo standing shoulder-deep in murky water, all within their own living environment. This was no zoo. Here humans were the intruders.

And some of the humans were rather exceptional looking themselves. In all sizes and shapes, they were meticulously dressed in ubiquitous khaki-with-lots-of-pockets and sported long, longer, and longest lenses for their Nikon cameras. Small clusters of them moved around in vans that popped open at the very top, telephoto lenses bristling in all directions. Most of the tourists were enjoying their one chance in a lifetime to "shoot" African animals in the wild.

"Jon, don't tell me you didn't bring your cameras," Betty nudged her companion when she realized that she and Jon were the only photographically unarmed guests at the Safari Lodge.

"Here? Are you kidding? My cameras are in the hotel safe in Nairobi. I've got more than enough rolls of exposed film to take home with me as it is."

"I was hoping for a few snapshots . . ."

"Forget it."

"You're no fun, Jon."

"I've been told that. Tell you what. I'll buy you some post-cards in the gift shop."

After their excursion around the park, they had finally returned to their rooms. Betty had just managed to get herself showered and redressed in clean clothes when she heard a tap at the door.

"Hi. Come in, Jon. Aren't these rooms great? My mosquito net looks like something out of an old movie."

"You'll be thankful for it in a few hours, believe me."

"I know. I would have traded all my clothes for one in Uganda. I've got more than thirty mosquito bites and I'm just praying the chloroquine works."

"It'll work. Ready for dinner?"

"Sure! Let's go." They crossed a broad lawn, heading toward the reception counter. Just behind it was the dining area, an airy room brightened by candles. Simple, well-prepared food was served in several courses, accompanied by beer, wine, or bottled water. The meal was pleasant enough. But once again, it was the conversation that made the evening unforgettable. After a few minutes of trivial banter, which concluded in a burst of sheer silliness, Jon suddenly became very serious.

"Betty, do you think you'll ever remarry?"

Wariness stirred inside her. "I don't know, Jon. I'm pretty much afraid of making another mistake."

"What are you afraid of?" His eyes were fixed on her face, and there was no humor in his expression.

"Pain. Failure. Devastation. You name it."

"Why?"

"It's hard to talk about all this."

"I think you need to talk about it, Betty."

"Jon, look! I've been hurt by nearly every man I've ever known. I've become almost cynical. I can feel love" (most assuredly, she could not deny the fact that Jon Surrey-Dixon had rarely left her thoughts for days), "but I'm not at all sure I believe it can last."

"In what ways have you been hurt?"

"I've been hurt by . . ." She stared at her plate, and searched for words. The right ones were nowhere to be found. "Look, I'm sure it's all been my fault. I wouldn't doubt that for a moment. But Jon, you're ruining my appetite. Why are you being so persistent?"

His lean face was grave, and as he brushed his hair back with his fingers, Betty thought his eyes looked unusually red. *He must be as tired as I am.*

"Why do you think I'm being persistent?"

"Because of . . . I don't know. Why don't you tell me?" She laughed nervously. "How come I have to answer all the questions, anyway?"

"I'm being persistent because I can feel your distance, your self-protectiveness. And I want to know why it's there. I want to know because I love you, Betty." He leaned forward, his voice softening. "And I want to know if you could ever love me."

In a solemn procession, all the men she had ever thought she'd loved before marched across her consciousness. Jerry Baldwin. Rick Remington. Carlton Casey. Would Jon Surrey-Dixon eventually join their grim company, the bearer of another heartbreak?

As was often his way, Jon seemed to read her mind. "You have to be vulnerable if you're going to love someone, Betty. You can't keep yourself safe and still find the love you're looking for."

"Who said I was looking for love?"

"Your poems, Betty. Remember your poems?"

Flushed with embarrassment, she shook her head, covered her mouth with her hand and stared back at him.

I knew I shouldn't have sent all that poetry to him. He knows too much about me, and I don't know a thing about him.

Half hoping to divert him, and half wanting to express a genuine concern, she said, "Jon, if you want to know the truth, I think I have a bigger problem loving God than I do loving men."

"What do you mean?"

"I mean, I don't really know if I love God. I believe He exists, all right. And I'm afraid of Him. And in many ways I want to do the right thing to try and please Him. But I don't think I love Him."

"Well, as far as I know, we can only love Him when we realize how much He loves us. And one of the best ways He's able to love us is through other people—friends, family, sometimes even strangers. But the problem there is that when people have failed us, we sometimes subconsciously don't think God loves us either."

"Well, the few times when I've talked about my fears of getting hurt by men, people have always said something like, 'Well dear, just trust the Lord.' I don't even know what that's supposed to mean. Should I expect God to force somebody to love me and treat me well? Or am I supposed to believe that if I'd just prayed, my husband would have been perfect, or my father would have been there when I needed him?" The more she spoke, the more agitated her voice and gestures became. Jon watched helplessly as pain hardened her face.

"Jon, are you finished eating? Can we go out for a walk?"

"Just a minute Betty. I want to talk to you some more. Who do you think God is anyway?"

213

"I think He's the Creator of the universe. I think His spirit is everywhere. I think He's . . . oh, I don't know. I don't even know what I think."

"Did you ever think about the fact that God *is* love? Doesn't He ever talk to you?"

"Of course I know 'God is Love.' But what do you mean, doesn't He ever talk to me?"

"I mean do you ever hear thoughts in your head that don't seem to be coming from your own mind?"

Betty stared at Jon. "Do you?"

"Of course I do. If I'm willing to stop and listen. In fact sometimes He gets through to me even when I'm *not* willing to listen!"

"I'm never sure whether I'm hearing from God or from my own subconscious or if I'm kind of, oh you know, fantasizing."

"Give me an example."

"Well, once when God wanted to heal me, I heard, out of the blue, 'I want to heal your skin.' But in the days and months after I was well, I honestly questioned whether He had broken through to me and performed a miracle, or whether I had somehow used my subconscious mind and simply healed myself."

"If it was all in your mind, why didn't you do it years sooner?"

"Yeah. Well, I've kind of wondered that myself. But that's not the only thing. One night when I was emotionally at the end of my rope, I heard some scriptures in my head that I don't ever remember memorizing. Another time I read a verse about the name of the Lord being a strong tower where the righteous could run and hide. At that very moment I was staring at the tower at Victoria Beach. I still don't know what that was all about."

"That the name of the Lord is a strong tower?"

"Yeah. What do you think it means?"

"If you marry someone and take on their name, like suppose you were to become, say, Mrs. Jon Surrey-Dixon . . ."

Great. Here we go again . . . In spite of herself, she was unable to stifle a smile.

". . . you would receive all that comes with that family name—both good and bad in my case. And, if you identify yourself with the name of God, with His family, you receive all the benefits that come with His name—including His protection and shelter. Just by saying, 'I'm God's child, I'm part of His family, and I need help,' it's as if you were running into a fortress of safety."

Betty shook her head, trying to process everything Jon was saying. "I'm sure you're right. Maybe I should just accept the fact that God gives me messages and tells me things."

"God is love and He speaks words of love into our minds. Just accept it by faith. That's all you have to do."

"Yes. I can see that part, and even when I'm ambivalent, I think I usually do end up on the side of faith. But there's another problem. Even though I honestly want to be friends with God, I've got to tell you—I hate church. I hate the people I grew up with in church, and the whole scene makes me sick."

"What kind of a church did you go to?"

"I grew up in a little, tiny Baptist church with a bunch of judgmental, ignorant people filling about a third of the pews . . ." She virtually spat the words out.

"Boy, do you sound bitter!"

"Well, I guess I am bitter. I'd rather be *anywhere* than in that church."

"So, why don't you become a Catholic?" Jon's innocent smile spoke volumes. She looked at him aghast, with a thousand replies swimming in her mind.

He laughed. "I know, I know. Mary. The Pope. Well, why not an Episcopalian, then? The point is, find a place where you're comfortable, and go there. You aren't rebelling against God, Betty. You're rebelling against people. And in a way, I don't think your disbelief is really in God so much as in the fact that you've never learned to trust in love."

215

"Maybe I've never really seen love . . ."

"I'm fairly sure, from what you've told me, that you haven't. Both fathers and husbands are supposed to represent God, and to act as symbols of His care, provision, and blessing. You've not had very effective representatives of God's love in your life."

Betty looked at Jon, desperately wanting to run out the door, and equally yearning to hear what he might say next. As it turned out, it wasn't what he said, but what he did, that concluded their conversation.

Jon reached into the basket of bread that rested on the table between them. He pulled out a single slice of bread and broke it in half. "I personally believe that a man should become God's priest within his own family, Betty. When he doesn't, everyone suffers."

He handed her the broken slice of bread, and poured a little wine into both their glasses. "Lord," Jon said, without closing his eyes, without taking them off Betty's face for even a moment, "the bread and wine are the best possible representatives of your love for us. We eat them in remembrance of You."

Betty immediately remembered the solitary rite that had sanctified her twenty-first birthday. At least this time she wasn't alone. She partook of those symbolic morsels, deeply touched in spite of herself, by the gracious way in which they were offered to her. *In remembrance of You . . .*

All at once, clear as any words she had ever heard before, came a completely unexpected response in her mind. "I have healed your skin. I am healing your spirit. Now I want to heal your broken heart."

Tears flooded her eyes—again. No way was she sharing *that* message with Jon! And yet, unsure of him as she was, there was no doubt in her mind that he would be very much a part of its eventual fulfillment.

Outside the dining room, three Masai tribesmen stood statuelike, festively attired in their red tribal garb and beads, their black skin gleaming like carved ebony in the twilight. With expressionless eyes, they scrutinized the lodge guests who came and went from the hall, as if khaki-clad tourists with cameras hanging from their shoulders were the most novel sight on earth.

"Why are they here?" Betty whispered, gazing at them in awe.

"They're checking out the beautiful American woman." Jon winked at her. "And, of course, they wouldn't be adverse to a handout."

"They're beautiful themselves."

"They come from a legendary tribe of herdsmen, a tribe with a noble history. They live on blood and milk, and consider themselves quite the guardians of the land."

"How do you know all this?"

"Oh, I once did an assignment about a Masai village, and . . ."

"Oh, Jon!" She turned toward him, enthusiasm lighting up her face. "Excuse me for interrupting, but that reminds me! Did you ever, by any chance, do photography for a *National Geographic* Ethiopian famine story?"

"I did some work there. Why?"

"The little baby that was dying—it was a two-page picture do you remember? Was it yours?"

He thought for a moment, and then nodded. "Yes, if it's the one I think you're talking about, I took it. But why do you ask?"

I should have known.

"Jon, I think that picture changed my life. I'm not sure, but I have a hunch I ended up here in Africa because of that picture and the way I reacted to it."

"How did you react to it?"

"By asking God if there wasn't something I could do to help."

"And you ended up in an African orphanage?"

"I did."

Jon looked off toward the horizon, a quiet smile flickering around the corners of his mouth. He was either unable or unwilling to speak for several minutes.

"Maybe tomorrow we'll see Kilimanjaro before we leave, Betty. You deserve a look at it." By then they had returned to her room. Jon glanced at his watch. "Look, it's early, but we'd better get ourselves to bed. I'm ready to drop, and you look a bit tired yourself. Besides, our driver is planning to take us out to see the wildlife as close to daybreak as possible. Could you be ready by six, then?"

"Sure. I'll be ready. See you."

Outside her door, Jon put his arms around her and held her close. She felt immediately safe and sheltered. He was the only man who had ever seemed to really want to know her, to honestly care about her. He was genuine and kind, and she loved his mind and his face, and . . .

Betty desperately wanted to say something to him. Something very much like "I love you, Jon." She knew that if she didn't bite her lip, the words might leap out involuntarily. But instead of words, she was left with only silence. Before she could resolve whether to speak or not to speak, Jon had kissed her very gently on the lips and walked away.

Her first hours of slumber were dreamless, and when she awoke in the middle of the night, Betty was at a loss to know where she was. It wasn't long, however, before reality set in. Some kind of animal was prowling around outside, rumbling and roaring to itself.

Sounds like a lion. I hope there isn't a hole in the wall somewhere. God help me!

She lay immobilized, afraid to breathe, cursing herself for even thinking about going to an African game park. But, before long, the threatening sound was fading away, and for the thousandth time Betty was thinking about Jon Surrey-Dixon again, puzzling over him and wondering what was going to happen next.

Should she have come here with him? Should she have rushed home and avoided this agony? Should she have told him she loved him?

She thought back to their first meeting and recalled the way he'd reminded her of someone. Who was it? There was a definite connection somewhere, like a word at the tip of her tongue. She sat up in bed and fixed her mind on the riddle. It was his accent. And something about his manner.

All at once, she knew. It was Dr. William Robert Harrington.

When Betty was still in the midst of grammar school, a fascinating new uncle had appeared in her life, newly married to her father's sister Gladys. He was an Englishman, a brilliant scholar, a Doctor of Divinity who was working on his Ph.D. thesis when he died. Betty could still see him in his V-necked wool sweaters and starched white collars, diligently pecking away at an ancient Royal typewriter, drinking gallons of strong, black coffee.

William Harrington was the only intellectual who had ever come within a hundred yards of the Fuller family. Harold had always called him "Gladys' bloomin' limey" behind his back. But the truth was, William was a likable man. No one had cause to disfavor him, except, of course, for the fact that he knew more than all the rest of the Fullers put together.

And it was precisely because of his intelligence, his unique interests, and his unfamiliar perspectives that Betty's recollection of him was so fond and so extraordinary. William Robert Harrington had taken little nine-year-old Betty Fuller for a day-long, whirlwind tour of San Francisco. Decades later, it remained the happiest memory of her childhood.

Now, Betty's remembrance grew clearer. Winding streets, flower-laden hillsides, and stately buildings emerged in vivid colors from the San Francisco fog. They had taken a ferry across the bay from Berkeley and caught a cable car upward into the heart of the city. There they'd beheld opulent hotels, a magnificent cathedral, parks, wind-tossed wharfs, and Chinatown. And then, as if he'd saved the most captivating event of all for the end of the day, William had taken the little girl to a Japanese restaurant for dinner.

Betty had rarely been in any sort of restaurant, and this one was elegantly appointed—even the chopsticks were exquisite. The two had sat on the floor, shoeless, and had shared the most uncommon foods together. She still could almost see mysterious little squares of tofu glistening on her plate and the laugh lines around Dr. Harrington's eyes.

As the ferryboat cruised back toward Berkeley, Uncle William had given his niece a silver charm, a replica of the Golden Gate Bridge.

"Oh, thank you!" she'd gasped in surprise. "You didn't have to buy me a present! The whole day was like a present!"

"Betty, I'm ever so glad you liked it. Just remember, 'Every good and perfect gift is from above, and comes down from the Father of lights . . .'"

"Is that a poem?" she had asked him, loving the sound of the words.

"A poem?" He smiled spontaneously at the thought. "Yes, well I suppose it is a sort of a poem . . ."

Dr. William Robert Harrington was no missionary.

Behind them, a million tiny lights lit the night sky as if a box of living jewels had been carelessly spilled across the San Francisco hills, their reflection spangling the waters.

Yes, that was it. Jon Surrey-Dixon was an all-but-reincarnate version of William Harrington. It wasn't his looks at all, for William had been a grandfatherly character, a trifle portly and a bit rumpled. No, the similarity came in his manner of speaking, the broadness of his scope, his *joie de vivre*, his keen intelligence.

And there was another thing. William Harrington was one of the few adults who'd ever really seemed to like young Betty Fuller. He honestly delighted in her, and when she used "big" words while speaking with him, he never reacted as if she were showing off. He'd loved and accepted her unconditionally.

In return, she'd absolutely adored him.

Then had come the phone call, and the sound of Lucilla's voice as she heard the news. "Oh, no. I'm so sorry . . ." William

Harrington had died suddenly of a heart attack. He couldn't have been more than fifty years old. He hadn't quite finished his thesis, and Betty was never to see him again. Her eczema had flared up virulently the day he died and had refused to improve for more than a week.

Betty shivered and glanced at the clock. It was just midnight. She pulled the covers around her neck, adjusted the mosquito netting, and listened for any further animal noises. Jon was next door. Was he asleep? She hoped so.

At last sleep enfolded her and dreams of Victoria Beach stole across the African night. Betty saw her tower, stately as ever, but strangely serving as a beacon. Even in the dream, she was surprised to see light emanating from its top. The strong, white beam danced back across choppy seas toward her.

Then, from out of nowhere, she heard the clear voice of Jon Surrey-Dixon. "Betty," he spoke with urgency, "do you see the lighthouse?"

She awoke, and it was nearly day.

What a bizarre dream, she thought as she showered away the sleep that still weighed heavily against her eyes. *I wonder why I would dream such a thing? It must have happened because I was thinking about the ferryboat and the San Francisco lights.*

Checking her watch, she hurriedly dried her hair and put on her makeup, well aware that the sky was growing brighter with every passing minute. She dressed as best she could for a wild excursion in the invincible Isuzu Trooper, pulled back the curtains, and caught her breath in wonder.

Rising above the arid Kenyan landscape, with but a single plume of cloud lingering around its snowcapped peak, was Mount Kilimanjaro, gleaming proudly in the first rays of morning sunlight.

At 1:00 A.M., Nairobi airport was teeming. Hundreds of weary passengers were lined up twenty-five deep, sliding masses of luggage toward six check-in counters. Elisabeth and Jon had arranged to fly together as far as London and to part company there—he would head for Kennedy Airport in New York, she for LAX. They had arrived an hour early and still risked being bumped off their seriously overbooked flight.

"I've got to get home, Jon . . ."

"It won't help a bit for you to worry. Just relax."

"Well I'm sure glad you're here. I'd hate to be facing this alone *and* in the middle of the night, too."

"You'd make it just fine, Betty. But I'm glad you're glad I'm here anyway." He smiled at her and gave her a spontaneous hug.

They were yet to conclude their intense conversation of the night before. The day had been fully consumed with a morning of sightseeing and a hair-raising ride back to Nairobi. Without time to shower or change clothes, the two of them were grimy and thoroughly bedraggled.

After two hours of waiting, wrestling with luggage, and standing around on the tarmac while the baggage was hand-loaded and unloaded twice, they boarded the big British Airways aircraft. Sighing with immense relief, they collapsed into their seats.

And so, at last the homeward journey was under way. Aching with tiredness, Betty dozed, then woke, then dozed again. Jon was slumped next to her, trying to concentrate on a magazine. "Boy, am I ever tired," she took a deep breath. "But you were right. It was worth it, seeing Kilimanjaro. I'll never forget pulling back the curtains and seeing it there, with hardly a cloud in the sky."

"You know, that doesn't happen every day. Sometimes weeks go by and the clouds never clear."

"I guess I was supposed to see it."

"Well, you know what the Masai say about the mountain? They say that he only takes off his blankets when good guests stay at the lodge."

With that, Jon reached over and took Betty's hand. He held it, looking out the window, while she prepared herself for another interrogation. Hoping to avoid it, she decided to question him instead.

"Jon, you were married before, weren't you?"

"Yes, for four years. I was divorced three years ago."

"What happened?"

"Have you ever read about the contentious woman in the Old Testament Proverbs?"

"You mean the one who is like a 'continuous dripping'?" Betty giggled.

"The very same. Well, you see dear Betty, I married her."

"What do you mean?"

"I mean that I married a beautiful, elegant young woman who seemed to love me with all her heart. We hadn't been together two weeks when she started in with a steady stream of criticism. She seemed to have only one goal in life—to remake and reform Jon."

"What were you doing that was so terrible?"

"That's exactly what I kept asking myself. And whatever it was, why hadn't she pointed it out before the wedding? It wasn't any one thing, Betty; it was everything."

"What happened?"

"To make a long story short, I withdrew, got busy with my work, and she ran off with someone else."

Betty looked at him with new eyes. "You must have been terribly hurt . . ."

"I was more hurt by her endless disapproval than I was by her leaving. By that time, I was beyond caring."

Betty looked fondly at his angular profile. "Well, Jon, I've never had to live with you, but you really don't seem all that objectionable."

He chuckled. "Well, thanks. But who knows? Maybe I'm every bit as disgusting as she said I was. The fact is, Betty, I think she was a little jealous of my career, my traveling, the fact that my name appeared under a photograph now and then. I think she was striking out because she didn't have anything of her own that made her feel fulfilled. In any case, I have to take a great deal of the responsibility for our failed marriage. I was most unsuccessful at making her happy."

"Being happy was her responsibility, not yours."

"That's an interesting way of looking at it." Jon turned to Betty and offered her a wan smile. "Anything else you want to know?"

Did she dare turn the tables on him and ask him the very question he'd asked her so forthrightly just the night before? Why not? What did she have to lose?

"Do you think you'd ever get married again?"

He gazed at her, the same intent look on his face that she'd seen there before. "Yes, Betty. I would marry you."

"But how do you know I wouldn't turn into a nag? How could you trust me?"

"Do you really want to know?"

"Of course I do."

"I believe God put you in my life. And I trust Him."

Betty was stunned. "So are you telling me that God's going to make me into the perfect wife for you, whether I like it or not?"

"No! that's not what I'm saying at all. I don't think we're all mindless marionettes with Him pulling our strings. That's ridiculous. What I'm saying is that He knows what you're like, and He knows what I'm like, and He was kind enough to bring us together. We don't need His help to be attracted to each other, but we do need Him to participate if we're going to build our friendship on a solid foundation."

Betty started to say something, then stopped herself. She was staring at her sapphire ring that twinkled back at her in bright flickers of blue.

"What were you going to say?"

"Oh, it's nothing."

"C'mon. What is it?"

"Well, it sounds a little silly, and I've never told anyone this before, but I love the poetry in the Book of Isaiah in the Bible. It's so rich and deep. And there's a verse in there somewhere that says, 'God will set your boundaries in colorful stones and lay your foundations in sapphires.'"

Jon held her hand in front of his face, examined the ring, and kissed her fingers. "Explain what that means to you."

"Well, I think it means exactly what you just said. If we build on His foundations, things are more likely to last. Careers. Families. Relationships. Whatever. If God lays our foundations in 'sapphires,' they are going to be rock hard and beautiful."

"So why don't you trust Him, then?"

"Who says I don't?"

"If God put you in my life, didn't He put me in your life?"

"If my mother were here, she'd say the devil put you in my life."

"The devil! Well that's an interesting idea. How so?"

"Well, first of all, you're a Catholic. Second, we're both divorced. Last, but not least, you consort with Pentecostals."

"I stand condemned on all three counts. But are you still letting your Mother act as judge and jury? Even from the grave?"

"No! Of course I'm not." Betty was instantly irritated at the thought. "Besides, I'm fairly sure God did put you in my life. It sure seems like it to me . . ."

Every good and perfect gift . . .

"Yes, I'm sure He did, Jon."

"Well then, why don't you just go ahead and love me?"

Her face was etched with pain. *I already do. Why can't I tell him?*

"Jon, you are the most wonderful man I've ever known. I think about you all the time, in fact I can't get you out of my mind. Does that mean I love you? I don't know. All I know is, I just don't want to play with fire and get burned again."

"Burned? Fire doesn't have to burn us. Fire is meant to warm us, Betty. It cheers us up. Sometimes it even lights our way. It's only dangerous when it's misused. You're the poet, silly girl. You should know."

By now hot tears had spilled out of her eyes and were drenching her cheeks. She shook her head, rummaged for a Kleenex in her bag, and took his hand again.

"Do you have time to be patient with me?"

"I have all the time in the world, Betty."

"You're right, you know."

"About what?"

"About vulnerability." She blotted her eyes again. "About not trusting in love and all the rest of it. I already know all that. I'm just having a hard time believing that I won't get hurt again."

Quietly, and with great gentleness, he brushed the hair back from her cheek. "Betty," he said so softly she could hardly hear him. "I don't want to get hurt again, either. But I'm willing to take that risk. And I'm going to wait for you, because you're worth waiting for."

They looked into each other's eyes for a moment or two before Betty trusted her voice enough to speak.

"Subject closed?"

"Subject closed."

Some six hours later, the plane landed at Heathrow. Jon was booked into one hotel and Betty in another, closer to the airport. Her flight would leave in the early morning hours; his, the following afternoon. Their airport good-bye consisted of one long embrace, a brief kiss, and not a single, spoken word.

The next morning, her big Pam Am 747 circled London and headed west. Pale and wrapped in a dull blue airplane blanket, Betty looked forlornly out the window. Once Jon had time to think, he would probably change his mind. And how could she blame him? And when would she see him again, anyway? Was their good-bye for a week? A month? A lifetime?

Why didn't I just say "I love you," when I left him? That's all I had to do. Why didn't I tell him? I'm such a fool . . .

Nearly paralyzed by weariness, by self-recrimination and

depression, she took out her notebook and slowly wrote.

> The streets were empty in the early downpour,
> As I, imprisoned in the inevitable taxi,
> Left a lifelong dream behind me
> Among rain-washed pavements, amidst huddled pigeons:
> You, sleeping under blankets of farewell.
> Now homeward I fly, through storm-weary skies
> Toward the unavoidable solitude,
> Farther and farther away from you,
> Silent in the London morning,
> Silent, somewhere just below me.

Betty read the verse three or four times, angrily ripped it out of her notebook, wadded it up, and threw it on the floor.

Once resettled into her familiar condo, Betty's sense of despair lightened. She missed Jon acutely. She thought back upon her own existence, before her time in Africa with him. The past seemed cold and unfriendly, like a black-and-white photograph from another era. His presence had painted her world with rich colors, colors she had never seen before.

By now, she'd been home three days, and come Monday she'd be back in her cubicle at Outreach Unlimited Ministries. It seemed impossible, but she soon would actually be writing the book about the Ugandan children.

I haven't heard a word from Jon since London. I wonder if he'll call me. Or write. I wonder if I should phone him.

She pulled his business card out of her wallet, reached for the phone and picked up the receiver. When she heard the dial tone, panic seized her. What if he said, "Betty, I've been thinking about our conversation, and I think it might be better if we just let things be for awhile . . ."

Slamming the receiver back into its cradle, she busied herself with laundry, sorting out a mound of mail, and listening to the radio. Barbra Streisand was singing "I Am a Woman in Love." Betty only caught the last line, "No truth is ever a lie . . ." She frantically spun the dial, tuning out the words.

I'm too tired for love songs. Enough!

Betty's West Coast clocks were set eleven hours behind those in Africa, and her body was not yet adjusted to the time change. The result was a peculiar, fuzzy mental condition. At about 2:30 her doorbell rang and woke her up—she'd fallen asleep sitting in a chair. She opened the door to find a Federal Express delivery man outside, holding an airpak. "Are you Miss Casey?"

"Yes."

"Sign here, please"

Who would be sending me an overnight package?

She glanced at the airbill. "Jon Surrey-Dixon . . ."

Mesmerized, she rushed into her living room and ripped the red, white, and blue packaging to shreds. A small box fell into her lap.

Unwrapping it frantically, she pulled out a tiny folded note. "Betty, you already have a sapphire ring. Here are your colorful stones. I love you. Jon."

Inside the jeweler's box glimmered a gold heart-shaped locket, set with a tiny emerald, sapphire, and ruby. A gold chain looped through it. Betty dumped everything on the floor, and ran into the bathroom to fasten it around her neck. It was the most beautiful necklace she'd ever seen.

She tried to call him, to say thank you, but there was no answer. She tried all day and all evening. Where was he?

Why on earth doesn't he have an answering machine?

Finally, unable to keep her eyes open for another moment, she climbed into bed and fell into a sound sleep. Then, at precisely 2:00 in the afternoon, Africa time, she woke up, wide-eyed and alert.

Smiling as she remembered Jon's gift, she touched her throat to make sure the heart was still there. She lifted her hand into the pale moonlight and turned the sapphire until it sparkled. She would have enjoyed its blue radiance more if it hadn't been for the horrible condition of her hands.

Boy, do I need a manicure.

Her nails were utterly ragged, and mosquito bites still swelled in red lumps. She thought of Jon, and the way he had kissed her fingers on the flight to London. All at once she recalled her dream about the lighthouse.

I need to tell him . . .

She glanced at the clock—3:00 A.M. It was nearly sun up in New York. Was he there? Should she call and wake him?

She studied her hands again, remembering the warmth with which he'd held them. She recalled his words, his patience with her. All at once she bounded out of bed and flipped on the light.

I'll write him a poem—that's what I'll do. And I'll Fed Ex it to him tomorrow. I've got to tell him . . .

Wrapped in a threadbare terry cloth robe, shaky with nervousness and cold, Elisabeth Casey composed a short note. She folded a poem inside it, and slipped it into an envelope. Before she went back to bed, she pulled it out, and read it to herself one last time.

Dear Jon,

There's only one thing more beautiful than the locket, and that's the fact that you sent it to me. You, yourself, are a gift to me, Jon—a gift from God—and I thank Him for you everyday.

In Amboseli, I had an odd dream about a lighthouse. With that in mind, I wrote this poem for you. I've never yet sent you a poem about yourself, and I really hope you'll like it. I do know you'll understand.

I can't wait to see you again. I love you, Jon.

Betty

P.S. Did I ever tell you that you remind me of Dr. William Robert Harrington?

Last night I dreamed of open seas,
Of breakers, surging swells.
An icy mist dripped down my face,
The wind was stiff, my little skiff
Was small and frail, wild-tempest blown,
And I was very much alone.
I blinked away the stinging spray
In time to see a star;
No, not a star at all. A light!
It grew from dim to clear and bright—
It was a tower, crowned by a flame.
I heard your voice, I heard my name.

"Where have you been?
Why did you roam?
The harbour's here,
And you are home."